A Feast
of Brief
Hopes

Essential Prose Series 144

Canada Council **Conseil des Arts**
for the Arts **du Canada**

ONTARIO ARTS COUNCIL
CONSEIL DES ARTS DE L'ONTARIO

an Ontario government agency
un organisme du gouvernement de l'Ontario

Canadä

Guernica Editions Inc. acknowledges the support of the Canada Council
for the Arts and the Ontario Arts Council. The Ontario Arts Council
is an agency of the Government of Ontario.

We acknowledge the financial support of the Government of Canada.

A Feast of Brief Hopes

Bruce Meyer

GUERNICA
EDITIONS
TORONTO • BUFFALO • LANCASTER (U.K.)
2018

Michael Mirolla, editor
David Moratto, Interior and cover design
Guernica Editions Inc.
1569 Heritage Way, Oakville, (ON), Canada L6M 2Z7
2250 Military Road, Tonawanda, N.Y. 14150-6000 U.S.A.
www.guernicaeditions.com

Distributors:
University of Toronto Press Distribution,
5201 Dufferin Street, Toronto (ON), Canada M3H 5T8
Gazelle Book Services, White Cross Mills
High Town, Lancaster LA1 4XS U.K.

First edition.
Printed in Canada.

Legal Deposit—First Quarter
Library of Congress Catalog Card Number: 2017955485
Library and Archives Canada Cataloguing in Publication
Meyer, Bruce, 1957-, author
A feast of brief hopes / Bruce Meyer. -- First edition.

(Essential prose series ; 144)
Short stories.
Issued in print and electronic formats.
ISBN 978-1-77183-240-3 (softcover).--ISBN 978-1-77183-241-0
(EPUB).--ISBN 978-1-77183-242-7 (Kindle)

I. Title. II. Series: Essential prose series ; 144

PS8576.E93F43 2018   C813'.54   C2017-906455-X   C2017-906456-8

Wisdom has built her house,
She has hewn out her seven pillars;
She has prepared her food, she has mixed her wine;
She has also set her table;
She has sent out her maidens, she calls
From the tops of the heights of the city:
"Whoever is naive, let him turn in here!"
To him who lacks understanding she says,
"Come, eat of my food
And drink of the wine I have mixed.
Forsake your folly and live ..."

—Proverbs 9:1–6

Contents

Contents

Long Shot

They'd changed. A group of my former professors had invited me back to give the annual alumni lecture. There was a fragility to them that I hadn't remembered from my days as a grad student. They'd grown older. Some of my favourites had passed away. The city where I had spent my doctoral years was still an industrial town. I knew I was back in my old stomping grounds as I approached the bridge that spanned the harbour. The shock of nostalgia comes when things, preserved as they were, no longer seem familiar.

As we finished lunch I was invited to visit the anatomy lab by the chair, Bob Thurson. The idea made me feel ill.

We walked the length of the campus to the science building. All the way there, my host spoke to me about how much he admired Rilke and how he was moved when he read my discussion of the poet in my most recent book. "I love what Rilke said about nightmares and monsters," he said with his head turned to me face on. The sidewalk was heaved and uneven because it was late

March, and I was afraid I would make a misstep. He noticed that I was wary of my balance. "Ear trouble?" he asked.

I said: "Yes. It runs in the family."

"I will show you where the problem is," he said, nodding and making a mental note of what he would demonstrate for me.

"You know," he added after a moment of reflection, "life is an incredible thing. We're all incredible things, machines, biological units ... whatever you want to call them. Did you know that over ninety percent of all conceptions spontaneously abort themselves? There is a code to life. Everything has to play by life's rules or life doesn't work. Most of the time a woman isn't even aware that she has passed off a conception that was not working by the rules. You, me, the folks we just had lunch with—we're all long shots that came through. Ever bet on the ponies?"

I said: "Yes. I like to play long shots, and most of the time I never win." I thought of the Kentucky Derby a few years back when a big long shot surprised everyone and came in by a nose. A friend of mine won a bundle that day because, like me, he is a poet who can't get beyond the poetry of life.

"Everything works by the rules," Thurson repeated.

⬚ In the lab, students were seated at benches along the outer walls. Some were probing pieces of pink, rubbery material in trays of liquid. Others were turning over grey and brownish-red objects in their hands and talking to each other.

We took off our coats in Thurson's office. A glass wall separated us from the lab, but we could observe everything that was going on among the students with their specimens. The benches in the middle of the room were stacked with cubes of plastic and inside the cubes there were blue, yellow, and orange objects floating in translucent space. Eyeballs stared back at us. Ears floated and appeared to be listening, and a severed nose looked as if it was about to inhale.

Thurson handed me a white lab coat just like the ones the students were wearing, and I did up the front buttons. As I buttoned it, I remembered I was wearing my best tie. I tucked it inside my shirt. I was afraid it would get splattered in anatomy.

He told me to grab a pair of rubber gloves as we entered the lab. I fought and tugged before they snapped into place around my fingers.

Our first stop was a white plastic dish pan like the kind my wife and I used every night to do the pots that were too greasy to put in the dishwasher. The room stank of formaldehyde which smells a bit like dishwater before the rosy sunlight smell goes out of it. It is a smell just sour enough to be unpleasant and just sweet enough to remind one of summer.

"Don't you just love the aroma of the place," Thurson said, beaming. "I smell that every day of my week. It locks in freshness."

He reached into the dish pan and pulled out a cold, grey tangle of worried matter that held together in his fingers.

"Hold out your hands."

I cupped my hands the way I held them in church when I lined up for a wafer from the priest. It was a fresh brain.

He drew a long pencil from the breast pocket of his lab coat and started to point out the various features. "The frontal lobe ... and this is the pituitary ... and here's why you get ice cream headaches as the referred sensation travels up the nerves from the mouth ... and here is why you suffer from migraines."

I was holding in my hand not only a human brain, but everything the brain's owner had known. I wondered if it still contained all its experience—the joy and nervous fear of the first time the person made love, the memory of streets it had known, the tide lines of conversations, and dreams it had made for itself when it was dead to the world in sleep but still part of life.

And was it part of life now?

Was it aware I was holding it?

Could it be thinking?

I thought better than to ask him these questions, but there was one thing I wanted answered.

I said: "Where do our dreams come from?"

He smiled. "I could say they come from somewhere beyond us, but that's not true. They come from this part at the back."

I imagined someone sitting in their own brain, as if they were seated in the last row of an empty movie theatre and trying to make out the details on a distant screen as the images flashed out of sequence and the dreamer tried to make a story of them.

"Would they still be there, in there?" I asked.

"Ah, no, no, we don't ask such questions in here. This is a place of science. You'll have to take that one back to the English or Psychology departments. And even they won't have an answer."

"Just testing," I said.

"Test all you want. What we want to know is how things work."

I laid the brain back in its bath. It almost floated for a moment, and I felt, though I could not say I knew, that it wanted to come back into consciousness before it was submerged again.

We turned and on the counter behind us was a blue, yellow, and red bonsai encased in Lucite. "These are the blood vessels of the brain. The red ones are blood in and the blue ones are blood out."

"What are the yellow ones for?"

"Those are the vessels that feed the nerves."

I said: "How did you make this?"

"We took a brain just like the one you held. We shot latex into the arteries, and when the latex dried we submerged the brain in a bath of acid. The tissue melted away leaving only this beautiful structure."

It reminded me of lone oaks I passed in farmers' fields each winter morning on my way to work, an outline of branches and twigs casting a shadow in the drifting snow of the dawn's light. This *arbor vita* of stems and branches had lost all the dreams and thoughts that had once inhabited it. That upset me.

"It is sort of sad," I said.

"There is no room for sadness here. We are clinical. We are objective and detached. That's the difference between the sciences and the arts."

"Does it ever get lonely, I mean, just thinking about everything from a distance even when you are up close to it?"

He laughed. "No. That's when we turn to you guys. That's when we read poetry. Love poetry. The poetry of the soul."

"Ah, so you do believe in the soul."

"Only in poetry."

Our next stop on the tour was another counter where a human head, in Lucite of course, had been sawn in half.

Thurson said: "I understand you have sinus problems," which I do, and I nodded. He showed me the sinus cavities. He explained what the doctor had done when he straightened my deviated septum. I saw the tongue still bedded in the mouth as if it wanted to speak. I was fascinated.

Then he turned the half head around.

I said: "My God, that's my old super! I knew him! His name was Bill Howard. On summer evenings when I was writing my thesis, I used to join him up on the roof of our apartment building. We'd sit up there, have beers, watch the sunset, and stare beyond the steel mills and smoky factories, beyond the harbour and the bridge. He said he was leaving his body to science, and here he is."

My host's face turned red, and he closed his eyes. "You have just committed the absolute sin of anatomical studies. You have personified a specimen. You have not only told me his name, you have given me his life story. Now, I can't use him to teach because I will look upon this head as the person you describe and not as an intricate piece of biological marvel. We're going to have to get another head now. Do you know what you've done? I'm going to ask you to go into my office, take off the coat, throw the gloves in the yellow hazardous waste bin, and leave immediately."

I apologized to Thurson, but I had crossed the anatomical Rubicon, and I did as he asked, grabbed my coat and walked off to the library.

I saw my breath in front of me as I hurried along the slightly jumbled and slanting slabs of sidewalk that would be torn up by the spring and put back together in their correct, level, pattern. I knew the story would get around before evening about me being tossed from the lab. I felt embarrassed, but the questions would not go away.

I thought about Bill Howard.

Bill had led a rough life. He smoked because he said it was one of the things he did best. Cancer killed him.

We sat on a wide strip of metal flashing with our backs against the housing of the building's A/C unit. Every now and then, the motor would spring to life, shooting a column of hot air above us, and we'd feel the vibration through our spines, and look at the beers propped on our knees, and watch how the meniscus of our brews danced in the brown bottles.

He would turn to me and say things such as: "Yep, it's a hard life."

Off in the distance, ships were passing in and out of the harbour beneath the black bridge that spanned the passageway. Transport trucks flowed over the arch from one side to the other, and the sunset, in one rare moment on a good evening, would poke through the spans and struts and break the sunlight into an intricate web on the bay.

"That's life for you," Bill said as he pointed to the pattern with the lit tip of his cigarette.

Bill turned away from me. His eyes searched for something in the distance. I remember his profile.

The stars were just appearing in the dark side of the sky, but the afterglow was alive. A warm wind caught his curly grey hair. The hair and its curls remained part of him, even in death.

The last time we sat up there and put back a few beers, I looked at him in profile and I knew he was holding that moment in his mind because that was the day the doctors told him he did not have long to live.

He flicked his cigarette ash onto the pebble and tar surface of the roof, and said: "You know there's stuff that never leaves you. You keep it right up here." And he touched his index finger to his temple. "Right up here. You remember nights like this." And we clinked our beer bottles.

And as I looked inside his head, he was more than a piece of anatomy. He was a long shot that had come in. I mean, what are the chances of finding an old friend, or at least the part of him I remembered, in a maze of scattered and dismembered pieces? What *are* the odds? If they are terrible, I'd probably bet on them.

Students in the lab stared into their microscopes, or turned over hearts and minds, to ask the same questions Dante, Rilke, and my friend the long-shot bettor asked when he put his ten dollars down at the window. What do I believe? I'm not sure, but I'll bet on it.

I had looked inside Bill Howard's mind. In there, in the winding grey matter channels, I wondered if there were still flashes of his wife and his daughters smiling at him just before he lost consciousness in the cancer ward, the cigarettes he had lit as he sat on the roof after long, hot summer days of vacuuming hallways and cutting the grass and bushes around the apartment's street-front.

I admit it is a stupid idea, but there, inside the store rooms and closets of his brain, I thought I could see the image of my former self sitting beside him. I was looking where Bill was pointing beyond the towers, steel mills, and factories to an ore freighter riding high and empty toward a vanishing point in the afterglow.

"Do you see it?" he says. "That one, almost gone?"

"Yes," I say. "Yes, I can."

Girl in the Blue Skirt

When I was a young man I wanted to be a poet. I was not a very good one when I tried, and my appearance said everything unpoetic that could be imagined. But I tried. I sent my work to little literary magazines where other struggling poets announced their presence to a world that never read little literary magazines. In the back of one I saw a notice that a woman in London Ontario was starting a chapbook press and was looking for work by new poets. I sent her some of my poems, and soon she wrote back to me a very kind letter that she would publish my first cry of presence in the literary world, a little collection of poems I had titled *Tongue Twisted*.

When the book was finally finished, the publisher, a tall, blond English woman named Sheila, asked me to come down from Toronto to give a reading to a poetry club in a library basement in London. Sheila was a very pleasant person to whom life had not been kind, yet she bore her sadness with elegance and charm, and she collected young poets with a motherly care. I was invited to sleep on her living room sofa and after the reading we would go to the home of a famous poet for a party he was throwing. He had read my little book and wanted to meet me.

The party was in a large old house on Wendat Street not far from the university campus where the host was a professor. The walls were painted in a variety of bright colours which made some of the professors appear even drabber than they must have seemed in class. A small, be-spectacled, moustached man with a soft voice and a pale brown cardigan noticed me standing in a corner with a bewildered look on my face and came up and introduced himself. "Hi. I'm the host here, I think. I'm Jared Rooney but just call me Jary. And you are?"

"Delighted to meet you," I replied in somewhat of a state of awe. I had studied his work in my English classes and suddenly the poet had leapt off the page. I forgot to say my name but added: "I wrote *Tongue Twisted* that Sheila launched tonight at the library."

"I've read it. Very good work. I wanted to be there but as you can see ..." and he pointed his hand with the glass at the gathering. "Come into the dining room and get a drink."

As we entered the dining room someone grabbed Jary by the arm and shuffled him off but not before he called over his shoulder: "Help yourself. We'll talk in a little while."

I stood perusing the table and the array of drinks and snacks laid out when a painting over the buffet caught my eye. It was a large canvas, slightly abstract but with a tre-mendous energy about the brush work. A cow was jump-ing over the moon but as it passed the craters and seas the animal was transformed into a blazing meteor. The comet that the cow became reminded me of objects I had seen in the prints of William Blake. A balding, grey-haired man with a very rumpled corduroy jacket and a large, full glass of something amber in his hand came up and stood next to me as we stared at the canvas.

"Think it's any good?" he said, his speech slurred as he rocked from foot to foot and pointed with his drink.

"I do. I love the energy of it. There's a nursery rhyme core to the painting but the use of vibrant colour and the break with object form suggests that there is something raw and elemental and almost absurd about the cow and the moon and the distant earth which is almost the colour of the moon. It says something about where the imagination can take us." I wanted to sound knowledgeable, but I had the feeling I had just blown it and that my poseur pretentions to artsy talk had been revealed. He stood back and glared which unnerved me.

"Ha! That's my man. You're right. You're brilliant!" He hollered across the room, "Jary, this boy is a genius! He loves my painting. See how lucky you are to own it?"

I knew Rooney cringed because his shoulders went up but he did not turn around. He was deep in conversation with a white-bearded man named Earle Birney to whom I was introduced later that evening.

'You painted that?' I asked. He must have been amused at the note of incredulity in my voice.

"I, young sir, am not only a painter. I am a genius as you have more or less approximately pointed out." His voice grew louder. "This young man, ladies and gentlemen, knows the value of a good work of art. He is worth a stack of all you two-bit little sonnuvabitch critics who can't tell your ass ends from a railway station!" He leaned close to me and whispered: "They can't tell what's coming and going and it's a good thing they aren't asking for dinner." He laughed loudly and put his arm around me. I laughed too because it was a funny line and it said something that seemed true to me. Critics should watch what they eat.

Jary's wife came over to us, likely with the intention of quelling the storm she thought might break at any moment. She spoke to me. "Pat has you admiring his work. I like it too."

"What do you know about liking it?" he asked her, his arm now heavy around my neck and beginning to squeeze me too tightly.

"I have it in a special place in my household," she replied with tact and dignity. She turned to the painter. "Someone called for you a little while ago and said they needed to see you downtown this evening."

"Was it you?" he asked, leaning into my face.

"No, I just got here and met you."

"That's right. I have no idea who it would be. My friend here and I are just discussing what makes that painting brilliant. Tell her." I repeated my explanation as best as I could remember it.

"See!?" he said, his head rolling back as he stared down his nose at her. A tweedy professor from Jary's gathering broke off and came over.

"I'm heading your way, Pat, and I'll give you a ride but you've got to come now."

"The bother of it," he said, squeezing me tighter, "just when I make a new friend, a good friend, a fine friend, a friend who knows a good work when he sees it and isn't comparing me to Riopelle, what do they do? They shuffle me off." He downed the contents of his glass. "Hey young sir," he said as he raised my hand into his and shook it until I thought it would come away from my wrist. "Don't forget me. Promise? That's a pal."

As he was escorted out by the professor, I turned to Jary's wife and introduced myself and explained what I was doing at the party and that I was Sheila's new author.

"Of course, I know who you are," she said and hugged me warmly. "I've already read your book and you have to autograph it."

"And who was that gentleman painter?"

"He's wonderful when he's not drinking but a terror when he is. That was Patrick Eden."

※

Young men are hardwired to want to go in search of paradise. It is the one thing that reassures them that the perfection they possess at that uncertain age might last forever. Paradise when one is twenty-one and full of the impetuosity that comes from having just completed a bachelor's degree can be a grail that appears and entices in many forms: women, curiosity, drink, places, leader-figures, and even, though I hate to say it, profitable occupations. None of those things, of course, last; but don't tell that to a poet when he is young.

As I got older, I continued to maintain a passionate liaison with poetry but was constantly pulled in the opposite direction by the need to earn a living. I chose the bank. Banks will always be there even if my intense dislike of them is shared by just about every other human being. And I thought that banking wasn't that different from poetry.

Both are about organizing abstract concepts, and both are about using systems. T.S. Eliot worked in a bank. So had Robert Service. So had Raymond Souster who I got to know through poetry circles in Toronto. Banking was the perfect place to hide the social imperfection of writing poetry.

I got married, had children, and rose in the eyes of my financial peers to the point where they could trust me with my own branch. But when the economy started to tank and client after client in my office complained to me about the drop in their savings, I became very jaded about money, especially about investment funds. I began to write more poetry, not that it helped, but it gave me a release. I also started taking what little I had left over at the end of the month and buying art in on-line auctions as an investment. The prices for such things dropped as people became more desperate.

One evening I bid on two small canvases that caught my eye. They were by the painter I had met that evening at Jary Rooney's home. The item description read: "Own a little piece of Eden." I liked that. It said something Blakean to me. The starting bid was laughably low. No one bid against me.

In one canvas, an old man with a sombrero stands outside an adobe house. He is leaning on a cane. His face is a smudge, but he is staring directly at the painter, as if challenging him. What is even odder is that the protruding beams of the house, the tree in the garden behind the dwelling, even the rocks that clutter the street, are casting shadows. The man is not. The painter is saying the man has no soul.

The other canvas is more brightly lit. An adobe home sits front and centre in the frame. There is a yard, and walking across the yard is a woman, perhaps a young girl. She is carrying a basket, but it appears to be a heavy load. She is wearing a bloused white top and a blue skirt. The painting was sold under the title "The Girl in the Blue Skirt." The girl's back is turned to the artist. She is walking away.

I bought these paintings because I knew their story. The night they arrived in the mail, I set them up on my desk after the kids were in bed and my wife was taking a long bath with candles and a bad novel. I wanted to stare at them. I wanted to look into those two canvases and try to understand just what happened in the Pueblo village more than seventy years ago. The girl in the blue skirt has turned her back on the artist and is walking away. I want to look into her indifference to see whether it is rejection or suffering that makes her shun him. Eden has taken great pains with the brushwork in that one painting; such pain of detail suggests that the moment is more than real. It is a mirror in which the future can see the past. And the other canvas with the man in the sombrero and his smudged face? I can almost see a fingerprint where his face hovers in the bitter midday sun of that small village. I can hear the crickets screaming out their pain in the dry silence that is penetrated by a dreadful longing, a dreadful desire to shout until that silence is broken. What the artist is painting are two almost coincidental moments that transformed his life. Those moments also transformed Canadian painting.

❦

Reference books on Canadian painting tell Patrick Eden's story with typical dispassion. Born in Montreal into a well-to-do family, he attended university there in pre-law studies before dropping out against his family's wishes to become a painter. (Some of the books say he was disinherited for his refusal to follow their plans for him.) In Montreal, he studied with a number of well-known painters of the time, among them Arthur Lismer of the Group of Seven.

One summer in the Thirties, he packed a few canvases, his oils and his brushes, and hitch-hiked to the American southwest where he hoped to fall in with the painters of Taos New Mexico and the community of artists there, the most notable members of which had been Frieda and D.H. Lawrence and Dorothy Brett. He never made it to Taos. His money ran out about sixty miles from his goal after he had taken a ride down the wrong road. In a small Pueblo village he set up shop, hoping to paint and sell enough canvases to make the final leg of his journey. The southwest adventure failed, though the books do not say why. One source stated that he was retrieved and brought home to Montreal by a cousin after he suffered a nervous breakdown. On his recovery he refused to do object painting again until he painted the flaming cow that hung in Rooney's dining room. He fell in love with a noted Quebecois actress who introduced him to Jean Paul Riopelle and the revolutionary Quebec painters of the Forties who turned their back on the old ways of seeing and decided to invent an artistic and political destiny all their own. *Refuse Global*. Eden, at first, joined them in their cause but later fell out when bouts of drinking and violence led to more hospitalizations for depression. Each time he was admitted for treatment, he emerged a newer, stronger artist, almost as if the period of incarceration and care was a living death from which he would be reborn.

He relocated to London, Ontario, when an offer came to him to teach at the university. London in the early Fifties was a strangely provincial city that had collected one of the greatest gatherings of creative minds Canada has ever seen. Greg Curnoe and Jack Chambers were among the painters, and they were joined by an English professor whose love was poetry: Jared Rooney. London of that period was Canada's Concord, Massachusetts. At first, in this Thoreau-like environment, Eden was right at home. His canvases were selling for increasingly higher prices. His use of colour, texture, and a refusal to let form dictate the emotional power of his paintings made him a celebrity with the art crowd in Toronto. Everyone who was anyone had to have an Eden hanging in their home.

And then, suddenly, it all stopped: the celebrity, the appearances as the subject of CBC documentaries, the camaraderie with the local artists. Eden was suddenly alone in the place he thought he could call home. And as the gathering of energetic minds aged, as Chambers and then Curnoe met their ends, London became less and less the centre of ground-breaking work. The references declare that, after several alcohol-induced breakdowns, Eden found himself single, friendless, and unemployable by the university. Yet he continued to paint. As is the case with so many artists and writers, a great silence fell upon his life. There are two responses to such a moment in an artist's life. The artist can crumble and wallow in his loss or he can reinvent himself. The latter is what Eden did.

In the Nineties when I was still a hack banker counting out fives and tens for old Italian women at a branch on College Street West and listening as they waved their hands and complained about the cost of produce and how their children did not come by enough to see them, I had a membership at the Art Gallery of Ontario. I bought the membership because someone told me it would be a good way to meet women—women who usually ran from me the first moment they heard I wrote poetry as a past-time—but they were all out of my league. Rich society girls do not want to hang out with bank tellers and they were even more disappointed if I told them I was a fortune teller. Still, I loved the art, spent many winter afternoons wandering among the Renaissance masters, and the gala show openings had great food and free wine.

A card arrived in my mail one day to invite me to the opening gala for a retrospective of the work of Patrick Eden. He had been rediscovered again. I stood on the top tier of the central court of the AGO. The Roman feeling of a sunken garden surrounded by stone arches clashed with the names of Canadian Indigenous peoples written around the cornice. A microphone came on and the gathering fell silent. The Director of the gallery said some of the typical plaudits about the greatness of the artist and what a privilege and honour it was to host a major retrospective of Eden's work. Then a famous novelist who was known more for the suffering tone of his sonorous semi-English voice spoke at length about Eden's hardship and travails and how he had bled, yes bled, for his art for so many years, and how that pain and torture had charted a new vision for those on the Canadian arts landscape.

After a woman spoke glowingly about the wonder of the sponsors for the evening's events and for the show, the proceedings were handed over to the painter.

There was a moment of silence. He began to speak but his voice faltered after the "Good evening ladies and gentlemen ... I am honoured to be here ..." Several people among the assembled coughed nervously. His hand went up to his bald head and he looked at the Director and the novelist who offered no assistance to his trembling efforts.

He began again. "Okay. I'm not a genius. But there is one question I am tired of answering. Two maybe. I can't stop painting. Only my death will stop me from painting. I hate painting as much as I hate answering questions about what art means to me. It is an addiction and I can't stop, so please don't ask about that anymore." There was a burst of cautious laughter from the art-goers. "No, it's not funny. It is tough. I can't paint objects anymore. And here is my answer to the second question which I am continually asked and I don't want to talk about anymore after this evening. Why do I paint abstract paintings? I'll tell you.

"In the summer after my first year of studies at the art college where I had studied with Arthur Lismer, I decided I would go off and try to find my way in the world as a painter. I hitchhiked through America. It was the middle of the Great Depression and I saw some terrible things. Poverty. Suffering. Desperation. But I also saw light and I followed that light westward until I reached a place where I ran out of money and where the light was good enough to discover things by. The place where my money ran out was a small village of adobe buildings. It wasn't Taos but it was good enough for me and I decided that not having other artists around might be a blessing. I'd have air to breathe.

"I found a room and started painting the town—both literally and figuratively. I was in the market place one day —it wasn't much of a market ... just a couple of women and old men with blankets and wares spread on the ground. I bent down to examine some tomatoes and when I stood up I was looking directly into the deep brown eyes of a beautiful woman. Her name was Vincenta. Just about every artist has a Vincenta in his life. That type of woman is what artists live and die for. They suffer for her. As Robert Graves would say, she is their goddess. Every day I would go to the market and speak with her and eventually she spoke back to me. She told me she lived on the edge of town and I walked her home one afternoon. She also told me I should be wearing a hat. The sun in that part of the world is unmerciful and aside from the headaches I didn't think about having to wear one. She took pity on me one day and brought me one of her father's. I'd have to say I was in love.

"One evening I came home and found that my landlady had seized my canvases. They were all I had. She said I owed her money, and I did. I told her that I would sell the canvases and pay her but she would have no part of it. I watched a few days later as her husband used some of them to patch the roof. I had nowhere to go, but at least I had Vincenta and I had some card stock that came from a sketch book I tore up so I continued to paint on those. Vincenta let me sleep in a shed behind her house and she would smuggle out their leftover bread and other things for me to eat. An angel is someone who will be there to help you, someone who will listen to you and appreciate your ideas even if they don't completely understand them. It's patience. Maybe the most pure form of patience one can know.

"One night I took Vincenta for a walk. It wasn't far from her house, just out in the back forty of her father's property. She told me her father was a very stern man, crippled in one leg, easily angered, and very possessive of her. My Spanish wasn't very good but I told her how much I loved her and that she had to be mine, somehow she had to be mine. She asked me how much I loved her and I responded that I would jump over the moon for her. Like the cow, I added. She didn't understand. I told her I wanted to run away with her and this frightened her. She had never been farther than her village. I was about to kiss her. I was looking into those beautiful brown eyes when she heard her father call. She turned and ran.

"The next day I was walking through the town and an old man on a cane came up to me shouting something I did not understand. He knocked my hat into the dirt and spat on my shoes. He seized my box of paints and opened them and flung them into the dust. Some of my work blew away, swirling on dust devils in the midday sun. He broke into English momentarily saying I, Augustino, curse you. You will not have my daughter! Diablo! That was all he said. That was the end of it. I ran after him trying to plead my case, but he just kept walking and without looking at me, blocking me with his cane.

"I had nowhere to go, nothing to eat. And no hat. I picked up my colours and the two remaining cards and reassembled my box. I immediately sat down in the dirt and painted a small study of the old man with the cane, a pueblo building in front of which our dramatic moment had taken place. I finished it. It was the only thing I could say. As the colours set I put the tip of my finger on his face and said: *Silence old man. You have forgotten what love is.*

"Then, for the remainder of the scorching afternoon I stood in front of Vincenta's house. I felt my brains boiling in that merciless sun. I thirsted, God how I thirsted. I was determined that I would die for paradise if need be. I painted Vincenta's house, but not with the rushed brush strokes that I had used to paint her father but with my finest brush, detail by detail. Suddenly Vincenta walked by me. I called to her and pleaded to stop and turn to me but she did not return my gaze. She was carrying a heavy load, bent over. I don't know what it was. The wind came up and her white blouse billowed and her blue skirt waved back at me in the breeze as if the tips of her garment were reaching out to touch me just one last time, and it broke my heart. I stood there and painted and painted until my eyes went blind in the sun and I collapsed, gasping and writhing in the sand. I don't remember anything after that.

"The next thing I knew I was in my cousin's car and we were somewhere in Missouri on the road back to Montreal. When I got home, they put me in a hospital on the recommendation of a doctor from Albuquerque who, unbeknownst to me, had treated me for a week and a half in New Mexico. My regret from the whole experience is not merely the loss of Vincenta, though I don't think she could have stood me for long, but the loss of those paintings that I did in the desert heat, my head boiling, and my soul coming apart before man and God. Someone stole every goddamned one of them and to this day I have no idea where they went. I went back there in 1982 to see if Vincenta was still around and to see if my paintings were still up on the landlady's roof. The place had almost disappeared. I asked and no one, not even the old people, remembered the woman I had loved or my time painting there until every ounce of vision in me was spent. I suspect my work that probably patched someone's roof ended up heating someone's home on a frigid desert night.

"As you can see, I recovered, but I could never paint objects again. Things of this world, even things we cannot bear to look upon, are of love. But we never recognize the love that is present in the world. We only see what we want to avoid. We are frightened animals. When I was released from the care up on the Mount, a friend from art school introduced me to Jean Paul Riopelle who showed me that the conversation between the artist and the world could still be as intense but need not be about things, and from then on, I painted only one thing—a cow jumping over the moon. That was after my third breakdown. I have had five more since."

There was silence in the rotunda. Eden stepped back from the microphone and began to weep. The novelist and the Director stood and stared and did not know what to do. No one comforted him. A lone pair of hands, mine, broke the silence and began to clap. Others joined me. The clapping turned into a symphony of cheers and in a rare moment of Toronto exuberance, the invitees chanted Eden! Eden! as if a chorus crying for a lost beauty that would never come again. The party continued.

As the reception line of Rosedale matrons and anxious

art world climbers cleared I stepped up to Eden to speak to him, but the novelist who spotted me for the minor poet that I am hustled him away just as I extended my hand. The painter did not recognize me. I was just another face in the crowd who had heard the story of a suffering artist. But I remembered it. That is why I own "The Girl in the Blue Skirt," and its companion painting, "Old Man with a Stick." I hung them on my wall the evening they arrived to keep as my secret. Two of Eden's missing works were mine, and they were the missing pieces in the puzzle of his biography. The tap of my hammer woke my three-year-old. I heard her stirring in her tiny cot.

"Are you still awake?" I asked.

"I can't sleep. Tell me a story."

"How about something shorter?"

"Tell me a nursery rhyme about a cow."

"Okay. Hey diddle, diddle, the cat and the fiddle, the cow jumped over the moon. The little dog laughed to see such a sight, and the dish ran away with the spoon. Now go to sleep."

"Thank you," she said and shut her eyes. "I can see the moon and the cow," and she smiled because it was true to her in a way that could no longer be true to me.

Early in the new century, I opened *The Globe and Mail* one morning while I was wedged in a crowded subway car's back corner, and read of Patrick Eden's passing. His obit was as tidy as the information in a reference book —cold, clinical, accurate and factual. It was not the man who was being remembered but the trail the man had left behind, the works that had been caught on a wind and carried beyond the artist. I took the obit out of my desk drawer and re-examined it that night I opened the package and set the two small, framed canvases up on my desk before hanging them on my wall. I did not know who or what I was searching for. And then it dawned on me.

Patrick Eden had transformed not only the art world in English Canada but the way English Canada sought to express itself, in much the same way that the Group of Seven and his teacher, Arthur Lismer, decades earlier, had transformed the whole question of who we are and how we picture ourselves in our collective imagination.

I wished I had done that. The poet in me, the failed poet who has never been prepared to make that kind of sacrifice for his art, admires those who could. Patrick Eden was one of them. And as I studied the old man with his cane, probably shouting obscenities at Eden in a language that Eden could not understand, I saw a fragment of something larger. That girl in the blue skirt, I realized, was not merely a woman turning her back on a young man she wanted to love and had to deny, but a link between two worlds, two ways of seeing. She was the key that unlocked the abstract vision to a whole nation that had never looked at life that way before, or at colour, or at that uneasy beauty that dwells in the troubled heart and has no way of declaring itself. Had she not turned her back on Eden even as he stood there pouring his love into every brush stroke in a desperate attempt to explain the tragedy of his own heart, someone else would have found a way to express that new vision that reached beyond the things of this world and leapt into the starry spheres.

So there she is on the wall of my tiny home office, a girl walking away, breaking a young man's heart, and changing that young man in a way that made him change things he did not realize he could alter. He is the cow jumping over the moon, that strange blur passing across the pale sky of gallery walls, defying logic to achieve the impossible.

When Everything Changed

Nobody likes a winner unless the guy who is winning is doing it for them. And that never happens. So, when the ship comes in, it is not supposed to be carrying anything. Victory has got to be hollow or it's worse than losing. It's like the story of the *Mary Celeste*. Boat found at sea. Boat empty. What's up? Nothing. Good. Tell me more.

Hank, for example, could have won the lottery. Then everyone would have just cause to hate him. But Hank wasn't a gambler, either in body or at heart. Hank was an academic. Academics aren't likable in their own right. People suspect they know too much and are suspicious of them. They say things—because I've heard them—like "well, if he's got a PhD why hasn't he made a million dollars?" And they think his lack of success is hiding something.

Hank always looks haunted. I suspect he feels haunted as well. He knows there's something he's got to know and everyone has told him he should spend his career trying to figure out what it is.

He used to tell me what it was like to cobble together

a job as an academic. It wasn't easy. One year he worked part-time at five different colleges and universities. He rode all over the place. He got a letter one day and he called me because he was really excited about it. He said he'd been offered a job by a university in Ohio. Ohio wasn't a long way away, but the great thing was that he'd been offered a job teaching Creative Writing, though it was out of his field.

Hank was an Anglo-Saxon specialist and loved to quote "The Battle of Maldon" to me when we talked most of the night because we're both insomniacs. It used to get me down when he quoted it because it is about everyone getting wiped out. But that wasn't the point, Hank would tell me. It was about courage and hanging in there when everything seemed to be lost because something deep inside, a gut feeling or just a noxious obsession kept saying that it wasn't time yet and that things would work out. Insanity and perseverance come from the same place. I'm sure of that.

The job in Ohio seemed like a good thing. He'd even gone out and obtained boxes from the liquor store to start crating his books. Then he phoned the chair of the department on the Tuesday morning because the letter had arrived late on the Friday before a long weekend. Hank was ready to sign on and he'd just gotten through telling the Chair of the department how much he was looking forward to joining them.

The Chair was silent for a long moment before he told him that he wouldn't be joining the department. Hank had gotten the job because he was the only person to apply for it. He was to be a circuit professor. I'd never heard the term. A circuit professor. Hank wanted to know more but it wasn't worth knowing. He was about to be hired to go around the various prisons in the northern part of Ohio and teach in those prisons. Hank said he saw the cover of Jack Henry Abbott's book flash before his eyes. The last person had quit the job because they'd been stabbed several times during a prison riot. It seems the university in Ohio hadn't put that in the ad.

Well, I said, you could look on the bright side. Let's say you're teaching guys on death row. You might not have to mark their final assignments. Hank wasn't impressed.

"Hey, where's Bobby? He owes me his project."

"Don't you know? They fried him last night."

So, Hank continued to ride the buses and his neck got worse and worse and started to crack every time he turned to look out the window. The crack was so loud I could hear it on the other end of the phone.

"C'mon," I said, "you could be in an office like me. You could be doing something mind-numbing like spreadsheets and proposals for projects the psycho boss will cancel before you even get the thing from the printer. You could be wasting your life on a treadmill with nothing to show for it, not even a cap and gown and some graduate photos your students email you at the end of June and tell you they'll never forget you until they pass you by in the supermarket three years later and pretend they don't know you because they are aware you are still riding the buses to low paying gigs."

"Very funny," Hank would say. "Yes, very funny."

Hank was getting grey through the temples. He didn't look right. He told me he kept re-reading *Beowulf*.

I told him I'd left my boring office job one day for a position in retail with a large hardware company and that my psycho boss had put out word on me that I was crazy. "It could be worse," I told him. Hank's head was still wrapped around the Anglo-Saxon world, and things don't get much worse than that.

Years went by, and for Hank I suspect a lot of country-side went by. And now I can't bring myself to talk to him.

I hate the guy.

There was this little out of town college he kept teaching at three days a week. He'd be up at the crack of dawn and then home well after midnight and everyone told him he was crazy to be working for them. Hank used to say he liked it there. It was like going away every day. There was a lake nearby. He'd sit at the bus station and wait for the late express to come and collect him, and sometimes it wouldn't and he'd be stuck, and he'd sit there all night and just stare at the lake and he'd tell me when we spoke that staring at that dark lake was like Nostradamus staring into his bowl of milk or water or whatever it was because he could see the future there.

So when a Persian Gulf potentate dropped a bundle on the little college that was so far away I couldn't imagine what Hank saw in it, it went on a hiring spree and Hank 'arrived' as they say.

He went out and bought the biggest mother of a house he could find and he said he'd just rattle around in it because real estate there was a fraction of the cost of the city where we all lived.

That's when I started hating Hank.

I pictured him sitting there basking in all his crap and day after day the sun would be shining on his pile and he'd go to work happy and live to a hundred.

The gang we used to hang out with agreed with me.

His other friends started hating him as well. We suffered with the guy when we thought of him on the bus and stuck way out there in all kinds of weather. We really thought he was a good guy standing out at a bus station in the middle of the night with the snow pouring down his neck and a shiver going through him. That was guts.

A big house wasn't guts. I mean, what did he do to deserve it? The rest of us worked hard too. And besides Hank is a long-distance call now and the hardware retail business is not what everyone thinks it is. It is not what I thought it was. I can spend my money other ways.

Neither is Hank's world according to him.

He left a message on my answering machine not long ago. It took up a lot of chip space until the generic voice guy from the Midwest US who presides over my calls when I'm out drowning my lousy life in a bar cut him off.

Hank was saying what colour he'd painted this room and that room. He sounded like Martha Stewart. He sounded as if he was about to go out and stencil the driveway or something. He said c'mon up and visit me. Come and have a holiday because the sons of bitches you work for won't give you the time of day to relax and I've got a fridge full of beer. He sounded generous. I hate generous.

I don't want to be grateful to someone just because God dropped good fortune on them. Gratitude is a terrible thing and I won't thank the man who told me that. I don't want to call a guy who is thinking about paint. I want to leave him alone with his paint. I don't want to hear that he's finally happy. That isn't the way I picture Hank.

I want to hear stories that will make me pour myself

another beer and say geez. I want to listen to people whose lives are more boring than mine, whose girlfriends have also left them and whose families won't speak to them either because they could have done so much with their lives and haven't. I don't want to hear that some guy finally pulled it off and the change was for the better because that means that happy endings are possible and we all know that's a load of shit.

I want to pick up the phone late at night and hear the sound of weary sighs, the sound of someone coming home dog tired and ready to say that's enough because the world doesn't respect intelligence, energy and perseverance. And in Hank's case, he can go to hell.

With My Hat On

There is only so much you can hide beneath your hat. I used to get yelled at when I was at school for leaving my hat on. In the cafetorium when I was just trying to eat my lunch, the monitors—old guys who were washed up teachers from long ago—would walk up and down the rows of benches, and if they didn't like you they'd knock your sandwich on the floor and you'd go hungry. They were bastards. But if they really didn't like you they'd go after your hat. They went after me, especially, because I had my hat on. They'd say: "Hey kid, take the goddamned hat off!" and they'd karate chop me from the front to the back of my head, and knock my hat off peak first. I hated that. Then they'd go for the sandwich. The sandwich was no loss, but when the hat hit the floor I always thought my brains would fly off with it.

There is only so much you can hide under a hat. The Principal always thought I had drugs in the seams. He'd stop me in the hall, order me to take it off, and roll down the inner band to see if there were pills, or powder, or something there. Then he'd shove it in my face and say:

"Lafitte, one of these days I'm gonna nail you, you little sonnuvabitch." He never nailed me no matter how often he made me de-hat. I wasn't into drugs. I was into holding my breath.

If you hold your breath long enough, you get high. Try it. I've been doing it for years. I'm pretty sure I've killed as many brain cells holding my breath as people who drink heavily. The only difference is that people who drink a lot don't gasp. They just keep on drinking. They pass out, too, sometimes, but they only really hurt themselves if they do it on an empty street on a cold night. Like my Dad did when I was two. Then it is really dangerous. Me, once I hit the ground, the breathing thing kicks in, and I'm back on my feet and ready to go. If you fall down drunk, you don't get up so quickly. Holding your breath is way better.

On accounta my name, I wear Pittsburgh Pirates hats. I've got a collection. I usually wear the classic one, black with the big gold P on it, because my name is Peter and people like to call me Pete, but I tell them they wouldn't say that to the guy at the pearly gates, and I deserve as much dignity as he does. I get Pete anyways because they say I'm no saint for passing out all the time. I've got a white one with a short peak like they used to wear in the 1920s, and I've got a round pill-box French cop one with the yellow lines around the outside, and Stargell stars sewn on the back by my grandma because she used to say I was a star. When I was younger and went to a special school because they told me it was for people like me and I don't see the difference, they used to tell me I was special. I'm not special anymore. They tested me. I'm some sort of fucking genius at mathematics, though they refuse to show me a math book because they're afraid I might solve the problems of the universe, so they just keep knocking my hat off. I hate that. I've said that already. But I hate that because my brains might come flying out. I'm full of brains. I just don't use them.

There are people who are lucky not to be special. They knock my hat off too. One day a guy in my class, I think his name was John, walked home with me. He was really down. He kept saying: "Man, you're so lucky. You don't have to succeed at anything, and no one expects anything from you." I thought, though: "I expect something from myself. I expect to be happy. I expect to be left alone." But John just kept walking and talking the whole time. His face was like he'd gone to sleep because when I looked over at him his eyelids were almost down, and he kept staring at the snowy sidewalk where his next step would land. I said: "I'm not lucky. I expect to be left alone." He stopped and looked at me, and just said something under his breath like, "you fuck," and walked away. John hanged himself from the baseball cage at the back of the schoolyard that night. I'm sorry for John. I'm sorry for all the people who leave me. I don't really want to be left alone. I just want to be able to keep my hat on.

The minister made me take it off when my grandma died. He said: "A funeral is serious and you shouldn't wear a hat." I showed him my Stargell stars. She sewed every one of them on. Willie Stargell had about twenty-seven, I think. He got one every time he saved a game for the Pirates. I was only three when they won the World Series but I remember it. I remember the yellow tops and the black pants. My uncle bent down to me where I was sitting in front of the television and said: "You're a Pirate, aren't you? Name like Lafitte, you're a pirate just like those guys."

Later on when I saw my uncle at my grandma's funeral he said: "Loyalty lasts a lifetime. I was there the moment you started cheering for the Pirates, and you're still loyal, but be a good man and take off the hat to remember your grandma." My head was too full to know what to do. I knew she was dead and that the only stars she'd be sewing on anything were the ones up in the sky where Jesus lives, but Jesus never did any sewing, so I was told when I asked the minister. He just said: "Take off the hat now."

The Pirates never really won after that. I kept my hat on, and when they were losing I'd turn my hat around. And then they disappeared from Saturday afternoon television in the summer, and the kids down the block told me I was a loser cheering for a losing team. "Pirates do what they want," I told them, and they chased me home yelling, "loser, loser!" at me the whole time. So, when I got home I stood in the window of my house and took my hat off so my brain power would disintegrate them, and that night one of the boys' houses caught fire, and the firemen couldn't get through with the hose because they said the alley between the houses was too narrow, and the boy's room was up at the back. The street smelled really bad. My brain did that. I know that for sure.

I was really worried when I prayed for my grandma. My hat was off because they said I had to do that for her. I looked down at the stars all over the back of the pill box hat and I thought that heaven must look like that, maybe for her, maybe not because when I asked the minister what heaven looked like he said: "Son, there are mysteries even I cannot answer." But I know my grandma knows what heaven looks like.

A man came to the house and told me I had to go back to school about a week later, because I didn't really want to go to school, but instead just sat and stared out the window of my bedroom because I kept thinking about stars and heaven. I asked the teacher to show me some math, and she just laughed at me. I said I had heard about a man in a wheelchair who spoke through a mechanical voice, and he'd said on television that math was the way to heaven or something like that. So, she shoved a piece of paper in front of me. I didn't know what the squiggles meant and she wouldn't tell me, so I took my hat off. It was the yellow one with the black peak, the reverse of the one I used to wear because I wanted to do something to tell my grandma I remembered her. And then it all became clear. I knew what the squiggles were trying to say. The teacher looked at me and said: "You're a bloody little savant, aren't you!" I didn't know what a savant was, so I said "no," and just put my hat back on.

Then someone who said they were a Special Ed person showed up and gave me more math to do. I said I couldn't understand it until I took my hat off, and she said: "Okay, go ahead." So I took it off and the squiggles started talking to me.

I kind of have a big brain, but because I keep it under my hat it doesn't ooze out through my ears like the boys who bullied me one day and told me when they said they were going to hit me over the head until my brains oozed out through my ears. I said: "Don't hurt my hat." But they pulled it off and threw it in the ditch beside the road, and the yellow turned dark brown and the lady who was looking after me said: "You don't want that dirty thing," and threw it out. That was the hat I wore to remember my grandma. But even when it was gone and I had my other hats on, I could still remember her.

I could see her sitting beside her old radio. It was a big radio that stood on the floor. She was deaf and had the sound up, but it could pull in Pittsburgh on a summer night, she said, and she'd turn the dial and the radio would squeal and sound like sandpaper until we could both hear someone telling us what the Pirates were doing. It was late at night. They were playing somewhere called Three Rivers Stadium, and I said to my grandma: "It must be wet there," and she giggled then shushed me.

When I closed my eyes I could see the pirates in their ship sailing up and down the river, and the stars above them because they were going to steal something that was important to the other team. She leapt to her feet and said: "He just stole third!" Then there was a pitch and the catcher fumbled the ball and he went all over the place to chase it, and she yelled: "He just stole home!" I miss that old radio. You could hear Pittsburgh. You could hear pirates playing baseball beneath the stars.

I still have most of my hats. That's good because my brains haven't gotten any bigger. If they got bigger they'd ooze out my ears and someone would beat me up on the way home, but they haven't. I miss the yellow one because it kept my brains in really well. Some of the guys at the place where I work call me Pirate. I don't think they know my real name. They probably don't care what my real name is. They just say: "Hey, you're walking around acting strange in that hat again," and they laugh. I know they aren't laughing at me. They are sharing a joke. They tell me so.

One of these days they are going to tell me what the joke is. They say the joke has a punch line. I tell them I don't want any more punches, and they say: "Sure Pirate, keep your hat on." So I do. They don't think I have brains and that's okay.

I play with math at night. I know how the universe began. I have figured it out and even written it down. It isn't all that complicated. But if I showed someone they'd say: "You stole that from someone," because everyone thinks that someone in a Pirate hat steals things from other people like their thoughts, or their lives, or their home. I even think I could sum it up in a pretty easy few lines of math. I know my grandma knows it. She's probably up in heaven stitching more stars on the back of the big hat that is the sky. It is what's inside the sky that tells the story.

The universe started one night when someone took off their hat because they had such a big idea in their mind it had to get out. But I know if it gets out it would hurt a lot of people. The man who runs the place where I live told me that the truth hurts sometimes. I don't want to hurt anybody. One of these days, maybe after he is gone, I will take off my hat and think about the man in the wheelchair with the funny voice, and I will share the secret with him.

A Feast of Brief Hopes

I know what was left for smaller men like me.
A feast of brief hopes, a reality of the proud,
A tournament of hunchbacks, literature.
—Czeslaw Milosz, "A Confession"

For his fifty-seventh birthday, Jacob's wife gave him a scrap book. She told him he could create a record of his life that he could pass on to their children. She had dug a box of newspaper clippings and notices out of the basement. They were from a time when Jacob had been a promising young author.

One Sunday night after his wife had gone to bed and their old lab had curled up beside her, Jacob sat down with a jar of rubber cement at his right hand and opened the book. The blank pages spread before him. The story of his life had already been written. The pages were the confirmation of his failure.

Failure and success are often the same thing. A friend, a wiser, older man, used to tell him during the days of his youth that it would be better if he were a complete catastrophe than a false success.

Jacob had decided to dedicate his life to literature—not just teaching it or explaining it in books, but making it. He wanted to make something real and lasting. As he flipped through the empty pages of the scrap book he realized even false success had eluded him. He was, in his mind, a failed false success.

He stared into the box as if down a well. Somewhere in the murky depths, his own reflection was staring back at him. The clippings were yellow with age and had a dank smell. They reminded Jacob of the manuscripts in archives where he had spent so much of his life during his graduate study years. They were wasted years, at least wasted as he saw them. He should have been out chasing beautiful women. He should have been drinking in run-down bars with wise derelicts. He could have been a catastrophe.

Jacob's meagre collected works languished on library shelves. A chapbook here, a short story in a long-forgotten journal there. Those who knew his work as a poet and short story writer thought of him as a critic, and those who knew him as a critic claimed his writings were too poetic to count for anything.

What haunted Jacob was not the shadow he had become at the age of fifty-seven. It was the ghost of a young man. He saw the face looking at him from the clippings, and he saw it that night peering in the window at him, his hands tapping on the glass of the study. Jacob tried his best to ignore the youth. With the box of clippings open, he could no longer pretend that the shadowy young man could be kept outside.

The youth held up a sheaf of poems and pointed to them. Jacob did not want to answer the ghost, but as Jacob stared at the empty pages, he realized the young man was his own reflection. His past wanted to catch up with him. That night he invited the youth to come in and have a seat.

The young man was cold as he sat in Jacob's study. Jacob said: "How long have you been out there in the night waiting to be noticed?"

The youth shook his head. "I don't know. A long time. I've been standing out there wanting the answer to my question: Is literature *worth it?*"

Jacob looked at the lad. "Depends what you mean by *worth it.* I have a nice house. I've put my kids through school. There are men and women out there in the work-force who have jobs because I taught them how to write properly. Maybe that's literature. I'm not sure I can answer the question let alone have you ask it."

Jacob poured them both a glass of single-malt from a cut-glass decanter he kept on a small campaign bar. He handed the youth a glass and sat down in his wing chair by the window.

"Nice glass," the kid remarked.

Jacob said: "Cheers."

They sat silently together for several minutes. Jacob stared out the study window.

The young man said: "You still haven't answered my question."

"I'm thinking about it. Even knowing that such a question exists is heartbreaking in its own way."

"But you gotta admit, it is a fair question because—"

Jacob cut him off.

"Damned if I know, kid. Damned if I know," Jacob said. "If I was your age, yes sirree, I'd be up and at'em. I'd be ready to take on those beasts. Not just the guys beside me in the literary stewing pot, but the dragons. I wouldn't be hanging around some old fart wondering if literature was worth it or not. I'd be out doing it, doing it anyways. I'd die trying. Succeed or die trying, I used to tell myself."

"And did you?"

"Did I what?" Jacob asked.

"Did you succeed or did you die?"

"Why do you care what happened? In fact, why did you show up at all?"

The youth looked at the floor, then at the bookshelves lined with volumes of red and blue and orange-spined novels, all neatly arranged like soldiers standing guard over a mausoleum. "Because I'm what you used to be. I'm what you used to be before you started wrestling with angels."

"Dragons," Jacob retorted.

"Whatever. That's our stock response, isn't it? *Whatever*. We should have that on our headstone because it is the motto of someone who lost the ability to dream. Do you remember that professor we had during our undergraduate days? She was a brilliant poet. She won all kinds of awards. Then she ran away from it. We asked her why she wasn't writing. Remember what she said? 'I lost my capacity to dream.' She started watching horror films as a surrogate for her inability to dream, but the sad thing is she didn't write them. She just watched them. You're watching your own kind of films now."

Jacob glared. "And your point is?"

"You've already figured out I'm your shadow. I read it in your face. I'm the boy from the bottom of the box of clippings on your desk, a look-a-like from a dark lagoon. I'm waiting there, beneath everything. You imagined me as you stared at the blank pages of your scrap book. You thought of me in the silence of all those nights when you've sat here staring at papers you were grading, and trying to make trees out of the sawdust of the English language. I'm that itch you felt every time you read the Saturday book review section and thought: 'I could have written that book.' But you didn't. You still could, and, well, here I am. I mean, don't be angry at me. Be angry at the distractions."

"So, if you're from the past, tell me my past, where did I go wrong?"

"You gave up on yourself. You weren't prepared to starve. You had talent. What you didn't have was the guts to let the talent say what you felt. Instead you did the right thing all the time. You said the right thing all the time. Writers, real writers, the Joyces of the world who live on bread and shit in asshole places where a person waits to show up and learn a language they already know—that's what you weren't prepared to do. That's the patience of a soul a writer must have. You probably still have it, but you won't let go to let the truth of your heart and your imagination rip into the world."

"But isn't it all the same thing?" Jacob pleaded.

"Hell if I know. I haven't been there yet. Remember? I am you before you happened to you, if you get my point."

Jacob looked at the young man and wanted to admire him, but instead said: "Leave. Leave now. Get the fuck out of my house."

"So, you're not going to answer my question tonight?"

"Not now, kid. I'm tired, and I've got a lot of thinking to do."

"Will you answer it?"

"Maybe. I just don't know. Can a person answer that?"

The kid stood up, drained his glass, adjusted the belt of his jeans and nodded. On his way out the door he turned to Jacob. "You know, I'll have to come back. You need me to come back. I'm all you've got if you want a second chance." The youth stopped on the front porch and again turned to Jacob. "Is literature worth it?"

Jacob closed the door as the kid vanished into the night. He poured himself another whisky, turned off the light on his desk, and sat in the darkened room. The light from the street lamp made his leather armchair appear as if it was a dark, winged angel that had wrapped its arms around him. Slowly, under his breath, a sob came up in his throat, and then another, and another, until his eyes were full of tears, and he had nothing to say to himself.

The next morning, after his wife had put out breakfast for him and gone to catch the train into town for a lunch-eon, Jacob went back to the carton. He'd had a strange dream. He was on a purple lake, rowing in a small boat. Even the sky was purple and the birds were purple. And he heard a sing-song voice chanting with a deep Irish ac-cent: "I must lie down where all ladders start." His wife had snored at that point, or perhaps the dog had jumped off the bed. Jacob woke, and stared at the darkness. He heard his heart beating louder and louder, and then closed his eyes and went back to sleep.

He stared into the carton. Once upon a time, there had been a young man who loved words. He loved words so much his mother told him he spoke in his sleep. It was gibberish. It never meant anything, but random words, new and polysyllabic, would roll from his mouth. They were the first thing he tasted when he woke in the morning and the last known thought he could remember when he left the world each night. When he set words to paper or clacked them into being on his father's old portable Underwood, he'd found the first real love of his life. Words were the window, not just to the soul, but to the world. And he could look from that window and see each day, each small human action not as something to be observed from afar with a cold, scientific eye, but up close, so close that he was a part of every action, every thought and breath. Literature was life. His life was literature. They hadn't told him that at grad school. He'd had to find that out for himself. He thought about how he would answer the kid's question.

Jacob came from a family that loved to tell stories. Sunday dinners around the family table were gatherings where elderly aunts and uncles would not merely recount some event or vignette from the past, but would mimic the voices of the characters. Jacob knew the sound of voices that had been dead a hundred years from the way they were resurrected in stories.

His Grade One teacher asked him to write a story for parents' night to put up on the bulletin board. The story was to be glued to a piece of construction paper. Jacob smuggled home a sheaf of lined paper and wrote story after story during a long holiday weekend. He woke in the middle of the night to write more and more. He had never felt so alive. He told stories about things he and his friends had done, things they imagined and told each other. His mother found him exhausted with his head on the small desk in the corner of his bedroom. He had written so many stories he had run out of construction paper. When he arrived at school on the Monday morning the teacher called him up in front of the class.

"Jacob! I told you to write only one story, and you could only paste it to one side of each sheet of construction paper." With that she began tearing every other page off the coloured sheets. Jacob recoiled in horror.

Tears rolled down his cheeks and then he became angry. "You freaking bitch!" he hollered. "You evil, evil bitch!" The teacher walked over to him, slapped him across this face, and sent him to the office where the principal asked him to present his hands. He was strapped twenty times on each hand so that his palms swelled up and his fingers lost their feeling. That night Jacob wrote more stories, better stories. By the next week he had a book. He dared not tell any of his friends or even his parents about his book. They would punish him for it.

When Jacob became a teenager, writing was a sin he loved. He went off to college and sat in the back row of his History classes, pretending to be a diligent note-taker, but instead he was writing poems and stories. A good-looking girl came in late and sat beside him in the only available seat. His free hand resting on the notebook was cupped around an invisible cylinder he appeared to be holding. She put her finger down the cylinder and stirred it as if it was a cup of coffee. That was how he met his wife.

When they were dating and later living together, he wrote poems to her. He handed her his stories. At graduate school, he got a B on his first essay, and a B at grad school is tantamount to failure. That's when the poems and stories became less frequent, and his neck pains began as he poured over books in the university library. When the library closed, he brought the books home with him. When his eldest was a baby, she would cry throughout the night, and when the morning light came the only thing that could make Jacob fall asleep was the fact that he had read himself into exhaustion and his eyes would not stay open. Was that the moment the passion had left him? What had he received in return when he traded his dream away?

He stood beside his desk and dug down into the box. On the higher layers were clippings of the occasions when he was presenting the medal for the student who finished with the highest average in his courses. In another, a valedictorian had quoted something Jacob had said in class one day, a throw-a-way comment he couldn't remember making. The words had changed the student's life. What Jacob had said had been an accident, and somewhere, out there in the real world, not the world of the classroom but the real world where people work, and live, and die, someone was living off a passing thought of his.

The rubber cement had become heady by mid-morning, and because he was between terms, Jacob went up stairs and lay down in the spare room bed where his dog curled up beside him. He remembered Laddie's days as a puppy. Jacob had taught him to fetch, which Laddie seldom got right. Jacob had taught him to roll over, which now the dog couldn't do because he had grown too fat. Jacob understood the dog. He and Laddie were cut from the same cloth. Both had failed to pay the price for wanting to dream.

Jacob woke in the mid-afternoon. It was a hot day and

something had gone wrong with the air conditioning because he was soaked in a sweat. The young man was standing over him.

The young man said: "Hi."

Jacob said: "Hi. How did you get in?"

"I let myself in. You shouldn't work with that glue stuff your wife bought at the dollar store. It will ruin your brain."

"I seem to recall a young man who put back enough beers to kill several brains."

"You had more than enough to kill. Look where it got you." The young man paused and stared out the bedroom window. Jacob thought he could hear waves in the distance, but passed it off as the sound of traffic.

"Busy out there on the road, eh?" Jacob said, trying to smile at the youth.

"No, those really are waves you hear. You're sort of remembering Pendergast. Don't say you don't remember Pendergast. He always sat behind you in Chaucer class with a big bag of onions he carried around. Remember him? He was the class Byron. All the girls loved him until they tried to sleep with him. He was so fucking drunk he'd pass out or throw up all over them. He wrote poems. Good poems. Maybe great poems. You remember Pendergast. He hitchhiked all the way to Mexico, to Baja somewhere. He sent you a postcard that you threw away because you thought he was a jerk. All the postcard said was: 'Got high on peyote and drunk on tequila and had a shit in the ocean. Go fuck yourself, Jake.'"

"Yeah, so? What about him."

"You thought you should have been like him. You

thought: 'Man, that guy's a real author. A veritable Bukowski. An F. Scott Fitzgerald, only far drunker and less into the bling and glitz.' You know what happened to him?"

"He died."

"No, he killed himself. He hanged himself. He wove razor blades into his noose and when they found him three days later hanging in the middle of a squalid little room in the worst part of town he'd managed to almost cut his head off."

"So?"

"So you ran away from writing because you thought that is what a writer has to do. You were fucking wrong, old fart, fucking wrong. Writing isn't about the posturing. Neither is teaching. It is not about the *Masterpiece Theatre* study inside your front door. It is about putting words on the paper. It is about feeling the passion for life, cold, raw, dead-on, cold turkey, in your face, snow down your neck, sand in your mouth passion, and wrestling with it until you find the right words to tell someone about it in a way they've never heard before. What you've got to decide is not 'Is literature worth it?' but are you worth literature? Others half as talented died because they wanted to be like you or they wanted to be you. Are you worth the pain and suffering you are capable of putting into words? And think carefully, because my life, not just yours, but my life, the life you stopped living, is hanging on your decision, and if you die the way you have been living then I will die too, and none of it, not the reading, not the broken binding on old books, not an hour's worth of living, or an hour waiting to be born will have been worth it if you choose badly. This is the grail moment, old fart."

"That's bogus, cliché shit."

"That's what you missed. That's what you wanted to find. That's what your courage wouldn't lead you to."

Jacob was silent. He stared at the young man. The kid put his hands in his jeans pockets and shrugged. "So, I guess I just don't know the answer that you don't know. Is literature worth it? Are you worth literature? Are you going to be part of the conversation or are you just going to stand around making notes about it that don't mean shit? Was all that reading, all that learning, all that surrogate for life shit, what you were looking for, or was it merely preparation to help you find what you needed to see rather than what you wanted to see? Was it sustenance or merely a feast of brief hopes?"

Jacob stared at the floor for a long time. The dog got up beside him and put a paw on his knee. The kid had vanished. He wept into the Lab's neck as he put his arms around the old pet, and every old tear that had been inside him for years smelled of old dog.

When his wife came home at the end of the day, she passed by his study and asked why he hadn't started dinner.

"We'll eat out later," he said. He was typing at his keyboard. His desk was littered with pages of notes scribbled on lined newsprint paper like the kind he had stolen from his Grade One class. There were lists of names, and arrows pointing from one idea to another.

"Are you writing again?"

"Yes, but this time it isn't about other writers. It is about me. I discovered something today I needed to say, that I've needed to say for a long time. I'm going to need you to come with me on this one. I resigned from the college today. I want to put the house on the market and move back into the city, somewhere downtown, where we can be close to things—things that we can see, and things we can imagine."

"Ah, Jake, this is rather sudden. I mean, geez, Jake."

"Look, the kids are all gone. They've been offering me a package at the college, and I just decided to take it. They want some new blood in there. They want those eager young part-timers who think they can teach literature fresh out of grad school and who will end up teaching others how to form a sentence. My time has come. I've almost forgotten who I was. I am remembering now. You're part of what I was, and I think we can reclaim it together. I want to pass you poems when we're watching some awful community theatre production. I want to stand up in a restaurant and scream a sonnet to you at the top of my lungs. I want to make love to you in the corner of a department store, and then tell you how beautiful you are."

"Maybe not the department store stuff. I thought the next thing you were going to tell me was that you'd found a blond and bought a red sports car."

"I need you on this. I got to the bottom of clippings box and I found a picture of myself. There it is." He pointed to a yellowed clipping that was on the verge of crumbling.

His wife picked it up off the desk. It was Jacob, years ago. He was tall and thin. He was at a party. His arm was around the woman he would marry and build a life with. He had just won a prize. The caption in the clipping said: "Greenhorn author will set the literary world ablaze." And as his wife stood admiring the picture, she held it up to her husband to see if there was something left in him of the young man she had fallen in love with, the boyish scholar who said he loved her more than words. His fingers were poised on the home row of an old portable Underwood.

Then she looked at the Jake she still had. His fingers were flying over his computer keyboard, and the words spread across his monitor the way wildfires spread across a dry hillside and illumine the night with a consuming brightness, and more than enough tinder to feast on.

The Day I Was Born

"**Y**ou have very artistic hands," the policewoman said as she rolled my fingers slowly over the ink pad and pressed down on each fingernail to make sure the black smudge was evenly distributed on the record sheet.

"What makes you say that? I rarely get compliments about my hands."

"The fingers," she said. "They are long and strong, but have a fine, articulate quality to them. I see all sorts of hands in this business. Some come in bruised and battered. You can tell when someone has led a rough life. It isn't just the scars and the callus-covered palms, but something about the resistance of each finger. The person might be co-operative, but the psychology is in the fingers. Your fingers roll easily."

I said, trying to hold back a smile: "So, I'm not a hardened criminal at heart?"

"Definitely not," she replied. "You are a people pleaser. If I were religious, I'd say you have a good soul. Strong, yes, but good at heart." The policewoman added: "The Lord works in mysterious ways, and I gave up long ago trying to figure it all out. For me, life is just what comes along. Enjoy each moment. Don't ask for it, just enjoy it and be glad it happened if it makes someone happy."

"Thank you," I offered. "I don't often hear kind words like that."

"There now, all done." I was handed a wet-wipe as she fanned the fingerprint card, to dry the India ink fingerpaint. "You're now on permanent record. I see a lot of hands in this line of work. Those kids are lucky to have you."

I had told her about the writing workshop I was offering as part of the local junior school summer program. I'd come in to the station to obtain a background check.

"It'll be a week or two," she said. "These things take a while, barring any problems or complications."

"I don't have any unpaid parking tickets, so that should speed things up. I don't drive anymore. I'm a diabetic."

She didn't smile, but shuffled the papers together and clipped the fingerprint card and my mugshot with the forms I had filled in. "You're good to go."

~ I waited. A week passed. Then two. Then three. I phoned the police station. I asked: "Have I done something wrong? The school is waiting on my papers so they can prepare payments and such, and I'd like to know I can do the workshop before I put the work into preparing it."

The policewoman laughed. "Oh, if you did something wrong, you'd know about it. We'd make sure of that."

The idea struck me as comic. I imagined the police at my door as a voice shouted through the megaphone to come out with my hands up.

The background check was to make sure I was safe to work with kids. I was going to teach a group of ten- to fourteen-year-olds how to write their memoirs. It was something I'd come up with when I was talking to the summer program co-ordinator. The picture ran through my mind of the group talking about the good old days. The idea was supposed to be a joke.

Marjorie, the co-ordinator, had looked up from her notes during our meeting with a look of 'eureka' on her face. "Why of course. Why didn't I think of that? They'd love it. Get them telling their own stories."

I hadn't the heart to tell Marjorie that one should live a lot more life before trying to write about it. How could ten- to fourteen-year-olds have enough experience to make a good story of it? They'd all probably been on family vacations, and those trips would stand out in their minds, but I was willing to bet the idea of entertaining exotic experiences in distant lands, the stuff of great memoirs, wasn't going to come up during the seminar. I even wagered with myself that they didn't own a Moleskine notebook. The insert in every Moleskine said: 'The treasured companion of Chatwin and Hemingway.' Experienced memoirists, at least as I pictured them, had filled volumes of Moleskines with incredible adventures. Nonetheless, I went to the local drugstore and purchased ten inexpensive hard-backed notebooks that looked like Moleskines so the kids could record their adventures.

The image of a ten-year-old writing in a notebook while sitting atop Machu Picchu made me smile. I said to Marjorie: "Sure, of course, I'm glad you like the idea. Let's go with the memoir concept. Everyone has a story tell."

The class was advertised and filled quickly. I was terrified by the thought of working with kids. Adults? No problem. You can make jokes with cultural and historical references to adults, and someone, even just one person, always gets it. Undergraduates? They seem to know instinctively when a joke is thrown at them, and whether it is funny or an ugly bomb of a comment, they still laugh out of a survival instinct. Maybe it's the Stockholm Syndrome. But kids? They frightened me because I wasn't sure I could engage them enough to get them to tell their stories.

The background check came through, just in time. The kids turned out to be great. I simply shut up for once and let them talk. Man, could they talk. They were the realest people I'd ever worked with. They taught me about the honesty of experience, how little things, ordinary things, are special and real, and how as we grow older we cease to notice what is wonderful about life. Life, for them, was a series of unfolding connections and discoveries comprehended through an insatiable curiosity. I was able to see the world from four-foot-three rather than six-foot-one. In the end, it was worth the wait for me to get the whole background thing approved. I learned so much from those kids. Kids that age have the best minds in the world. They want to know everything that can be known, but they haven't forgotten what it is to not know. Maybe that's innocence. I call it wisdom.

They were good writers as well.

One kid had an imaginary friend. I suppose just about every kid, at sometime or other, has an imaginary friend. I had been a lonely child. I had one. He was a kind elderly man who knew right from wrong, and who always wanted to guide me in the right direction. He disappeared when I went to kindergarten.

One kid in my class, a young, shy girl who loved to speak in riddles, was very attached to her imaginary friend. Her friend was not very good, but the bad things that the shadow-self did made the real kid try even harder to be good. The shadow friend was a means by which she understood the things life asked of her. The friend made her a better person. I told her father that when he came to sign her out at the end of one of the last sessions.

"Wouldn't know any other," he said with not the slightest hint of reservation or even wryness in his voice as he shook my hand and thanked me for getting his daughter to love writing.

The days before the class began, however, were anxious ones for me. At the end of the third week of waiting for my papers to come through from the police department, I phoned the fingerprint lady and inquired about the delay. "Yes," said the voice on the other end of the phone. "Your background check has been delayed, but it should be through in a day or so."

I hesitated. I said: "What exactly am I supposed to have done? Am I wanted in three provinces?"

The woman laughed into the receiver. The laugh startled me. Had I scored a funny without knowing it?

"No, no. Nothing of the kind. The paperwork is taking longer to process because of your birthdate."

"My birthdate? Was my birthday a bad day for people in general?"

"Not for you," she replied. "For someone else, yes. They probably wish they had never been born. I hope you don't mind me saying this, but you'll understand because you're a writer. You might say there is someone out there who is the shadow of you, if you know what I mean. A dark shadow."

"That's sad," I interjected. "I mean, what could a person do that would put them into that kind of situation?"

"You'd be surprised. In my line of work ... well, you'd be surprised. Sad for him. You see we have to make sure you are not him." I was intrigued by the circularity of her argument. "I know that sounds odd. But you could be him."

"What would make me him or him me?"

"You were not only born on the same day, and in the same hospital, but at the same time of day. That's what the records say. You could be him, and until we prove you are not him ... so you'll have to wait until we prove you are not him."

I wanted to sing a chorus of that old song "I Gotta Be Me," but thought better of it. Sarcasm isn't a crowd-pleaser with police people. Back when I wasn't diabetic and had a driver's licence, I got pulled over by a patrolman who leaned down to my window and asked me, without saying please, to produce my license. I pulled it out of my back-pocket wallet and presented it with both hands, as if he was a Japanese business man. He snapped it out of my fingers.

"Was I going too fast?"

"You were five kilometers over the limit." He walked back to his cruiser and called in my name and plates. I wasn't who he thought I was. I was clean. As he sauntered back to my car, jacking up his trousers from the belt and adjusting his sun glasses so he looked completely official, an essay by Michel de Montaigne I taught my students in a composition class flashed into my head.

"No officer of the law is successful without someone to break the law."

The point Montaigne was making was that the world needs things to go wrong in order for things to go right. There is a balance to everything. Good keeps evil in check.

The officer looked in my car. I was ashamed of the empty coffee cups I'd tossed in the back.

"I'm letting you off with a warning this time because you've got a clean record. Just make sure you slow down and be respectful of the safety of others."

I was going to get off scot free when the bad voice inside me had to chirp up—and I hate that part of myself because I know it is the aspect of my personality that always wants to push things just a little bit too far.

"Glad I made your day, officer. You'd have had nothing to do if I hadn't been over the limit."

That almost cost me one hundred dollars. I made a point never to joke with an officer of the law again, even if she was holding my hands admiringly.

The policewoman put me on hold and went away to look for my paperwork. When she returned, she told me I had a doppelganger, a dark creature from the lagoon of the stars that had presided over my birth and my shadow's. I started wondering who that person was and what he had done that was so awful.

Stars are tricky. I read the horoscopes every day. I read them late in the day so I can fact-check to see if they were correct or not. I have an astrologer friend in New York who tells me that my playful cynicism is insulting to his art, but nonetheless I never want to bet on a horse until it has crossed the finish line. But the dark stars from the day I was born troubled me.

Whoever it was, we shared the same birthday. Given that we both started from the same point in time—the same day and even the same hour—what had made his life so different from mine? Nature versus nurture?

I stared out the window in front of my desk for several hours one afternoon and thought about birthdays. I was thinking about my childhood. It had been a very happy childhood. The birthday parties were special.

My birthday was the one day of the year I was permitted to have soft drinks. One of my friends figured out a way to blow Coca Cola out his nose, and the party came to a halt as my mother scolded us for getting soft drinks on the dining room carpet. The cakes, the candles I blew out in one breath, they were happy memories. Even when I was uncertain about life, the happiness of those days sustained me like a birthday cake of endless corner pieces. Those parties were expressions of the love that had shaped my early years. My mother went to a lot of trouble and maintained grace under fire even when things did not work out as she had planned.

I dropped by my mother's place to change some light bulbs for her. She told me what the day I was born had been like. It was the first warm day of the year. The temperature soared from a late-winter chill to a balmy, humid morning when the grass turned green within an hour, and the buds on the forsythia cracked open like popcorn kernels.

"The day you were born," she said as she set her cup down in the saucer—we were always the kind of family

that used cups and saucers because such things transformed daily life into small rituals—"it was so hot in my
maternity room that the nurses brought in bowls of ice
and set fans in front of them to cool me down. My blood
pressure went way up. The doctor was worried you wouldn't
make it. You were born at a quarter to four, and you
looked like a wizened old man with the cares of the world
on his shoulders. As soon as they let me stand up and get
out of bed, it was early evening by then, I held you up to
the window that looked across University Avenue to a
long-gone dead-end street called Ord Street. There was
an old black wrought iron fence separating the street from
the busy avenue, and all your cousins were lined up there
with your aunts and uncles to see the baby high up in a
window on the fifth floor. I don't think they saw more
than the blanket, but they all started waving their arms.
They'd made cards saying: 'Welcome to our family.'"

"Do you recall any of the other mothers there at the
same time? Were you comparing notes with them or just
hanging out and talking about motherhood and stuff?"

"How would I remember? Darling, that was over half
a century ago. Jennifer McBain gave birth to her daughter
Maureen the same day, at around the same time. You were
both christened together, and you used to play together
when you were small."

"Yes, I remember her. She was a very beautiful girl. We
liked to hold hands as we swung back and forth on the
horses of my swing set. I always let her have the white
horse because I liked her so much."

"Sad," said my mother. "Maureen died of cancer last
year. The sad thing was that she had become a doctor and

was an important cancer researcher. I thought I'd told you. I guess I didn't."

She was about to stir a drop of milk into the new cup she'd poured herself but stopped with the cream jug poised above the cup.

"There were mothers all over the place. That was during the Baby Boom. You couldn't walk down a hallway at feeding time without bumping into carts and carts of babies. I don't know how they got all the babies to their correct mothers, but I always knew that you were mine. You looked just like your father, only rounder and more serious. The others cried, but you were pretty good. So was Maureen. Jennifer and I both said how lucky we were. By the time you were ready to go home you didn't look like a sad balloon with the air let out of it anymore."

"I'm curious because I'm trying to find out who else was born in the hospital on my birthday. I'm unnerved by the fact that there's this person out there who arrived in the world in the same place and at the same time as me. He's held up my background check and probably a few banks as well. We should, according to the laws of destiny, share the same path because we share the same stars, but his life has been far different from mine. He is a criminal."

She said: "Dear, the fault is not in our stars but in ourselves. I wouldn't bother. It's like your adopted cousin who went looking for her birth father and got a very unhappy story. Whoever he is, he is nothing to you. I'd stay clear of him."

"He may be nothing to me except that the system I live in and work in and live by thought we might be the same person. People change their names. They can't change the day they were born. That's their launching point. Like satellites. Once their orbit is set, that's the way they have to go, or at least that's what astrologers say. I want to make sure I'm not like him."

She shook her head. "Darling, you're about as far away from that kind of life as a person can be. You've turned out fine. You've made your own orbit."

⮑ But I refused to heed her advice. I sat down in the city library and began to scan through the cards of microfiche. They were brittle black sheets with constellations of tiny white windows across them. Each window was a page of a newspaper, and each card held pages and pages of information about things that were important one particular day, and were now forgotten. Daily news. One evening edition from the month before my birth began to crumble as I laid it gently on the bed of the reader and slid the card beneath the enormous eye of the machine.

There were ads for chesterfields, half page displays of refrigerators. There were news items about "Eisenhower says this," and "St. Laurent says that." It all gave me a 'hell if I know' feeling as I realized I had lived my life in a state of historical amnesia to the minutiae of daily facts, facts that didn't matter to me. If I had to write a test on what had happened in my life, I would probably fail.

So, why was I looking for a person who only shared one coincidental moment with me, and probably nothing more? Was life the moment, or the sum of all moments lived? Was it the event, or the ability to outgrow or outlive an event? I looked at the smudged and faded images and realized I was older than I ever thought I was. I had led a happy life, but I wanted a clear view of a future I never wanted to give up on. I was an idiot abroad. Happiness had blinded me to time.

After about half an hour of searching, I found it. There it was, in both the *Telegram* and the *Star*. My arrival in the world was announced by a small statement that could fit under my thumb. A person gets sucked into believing the great illusion of life, namely that one should go out with far more column space than they got when they came in. Beneath my name I saw Maureen McBain's.

I remembered her hair. It was beautiful hair. She didn't come into the world with it. In my mind, aside for what else she accomplished, she had made wonderful hair for herself.

Some of the babies had been born at other hospitals. I could eliminate them from my list. There were two others that seemed to fit the description. Boys. Thomas David Cross and Michael Benjamin Thorley. I wrote down their names. On my laptop I searched their names.

Cross had been killed in a car accident. His obituary spoke of how he had been a teacher. He had worked for an international relief organization in Africa. He had come home, raised a family, and been a high school teacher. His community honoured him for his service. The story of his life talked about what a good person he was.

I felt relieved.

Just reading his story inspired me. This was someone I should have known. His students and everyone who knew him mourned him deeply. He had made a difference to the world. I wish I could have been like him, just as I wished I could have been like Maureen McBain when I thought about our play time together as kids and the research work she had done.

What was troubling was that people born on my day, at about my time, were not doing so well. We were just two of four now. They were mortal. I was mortal. Here I was looking back upon the first, important moment of my life, a moment I could not remember, and death walks into my imagination and has a seat in the chair in front of me. Life up to that point had been an *always*. Now it became a matter of *for the time being*. Thank you, Cross. I know you didn't mean to leave me with that.

Thorley wasn't on Canada 411 where lists of telephone numbers of everyone in the country are arranged alphabetically, so I Googled him.

There he was in numerous newspaper accounts. He had his column space, but at a price that others paid.

He was incarcerated in Millhaven Maximum Security Detention Centre—a euphemism for hard time—about a hundred miles east of the city. He'd done terrible things. There was an article about him robbing a senior when he was sixteen. He had knocked the old man down, taken his wallet, and even when the old guy pleaded, he had grabbed the man's watch. It had been a gift from the senior's father. Thorley didn't take it. He'd smashed it in front of the old man before beating him up.

Parole. Maybe someone thought his life would change. It didn't.

He'd gone back to jail a second, third, and fourth time.

Repeat offender.

He'd murdered his mother.

Dangerous offender.

He was freed again. His last crime was the murder of a child. I felt sick to my stomach.

My mother had quoted Shakespeare's line about the fault being not in our stars but in ourselves. I wondered about how true that might be as I stared out the window on the east-bound Lakeshore train.

I was on my way to meet this dark shadow with whom I had nothing in common except a warm spring day long ago.

I went because I wanted to prove to my friend in New York that he was wrong about the stars shaping us and making us who we are.

I wanted to satisfy myself that even though people are born at the same time and in the same place they are born different, that our paths only crossed once—in those hospital corridors where our mothers sweated and pushed on a hot spring afternoon because they were caught in the beautiful cycle of life. I wanted to assure myself that Maureen whom I had known, and Tom Cross whom I wish I had known, were their own people who made the world what they wanted it to be. I wanted to assure myself I was my own person.

I am tall and thin. I'm growing thinner, gaunter, every day because of my diabetes. I walk several miles a day to please a doctor who told me I could beat the sugar sickness if I lost more weight. My hair is thick. My body, the carriage of the mind and soul, is still in pretty good shape. I want to shape my own ends.

⌇ A door opened behind the glass wall. Out walked a man who was nothing like me. His arms were covered in bad tattoos. He was taller than me. Heavy-set. Bald. He was the cliché inmate, and something in me was glad that he was.

We didn't share the same hair colour, or shape of nose, or eyes. His hands were swollen, maybe from fighting, maybe from high blood pressure. The knuckles looked like walnuts. We didn't walk the same way, or sit down and rest our hands or elbows on the countertop the same way. I stared at him and he wouldn't make eye contact with me.

He said: "Who the fuck are you and what do you want?"

I told him the story. I told him the reason I had come to see him. We shared coincidental moments of birth. Had the stars made us different? What had been the point in his life where he turned on people to hurt them? Did the universe in which we are just mere specks of life make any difference to who we are?

At first he tried to follow my monologue. He even tried to mouth the words I was saying as if he had trouble taking it all in. Once or twice he nodded, and I thought, yes, I am getting through to him, but then I knew I lost him. He had me figured for a head case.

I had told him about the miracle of the day we were born, how the forsythia all over the city had sprung with a great shout of yellow to proclaim life.

He looked at me as if I had just spoken an ancient language and he didn't catch a word.

"Fuck you," he said, and stood up and left. The door closed behind him and the matter was settled.

Okay, I thought, as I sat there for a moment and collected my thoughts. I probably am some kind of looney he spotted me for. What else did I expect? What was I looking for?

Maybe he might have told me his life story, but why should he? I meant nothing to him. His life was his, and mine was mine.

I realized I was a complete ass. I'd come all the way to his jail because I wanted to know, to know for certain, that he was not me. Telling him about my life ticked him off. I don't blame him. Happiness can make a person insensitive. My Mom was right. I should have left it all alone.

He was not even my bad shadow. The two of us had gone our separate ways from the one moment we had in common.

I rode the westbound train back to the city, and the sunset glowed orange with the last life of the day still ahead of me. The first evening stars appeared over the lake. I turned around in my seat and looked at what my journey was leaving behind.

If I ever wrote my life story it would contain that moment. The eastern sky had become ink-blue, and its darkness receded into the past.

Instruction

Y ou will be seated in a small, dark box for the final act of your passage into a new name. A voice will come to you out of the darkness and ask you questions you might not be able to answer in daylight. That is why it will be dark.

Are you prepared to walk into a place deep inside you did not know was there until now, and where even you have avoided going for fear of the answers you might find there? You may have lived your entire life without knowing that place is inside you.

You will find yourself in the death that has always been inside you. Is it merely a closet where you have hidden things that you promised yourself you would deal with someday, if you had the time?

Are you prepared to walk into the centre of your being and its darkness and find the answers there?

Do you have the power within yourself to let that place speak for you?

That is how the process ends. You will need to remind

yourself how it all began and why you undertook the journey to such a dark place.

～ The first step in the process of becoming a new person, of possessing that new name, is just as hard. Are you aware of the step you are about to undertake? Think carefully. You will be told it is a step not to be taken lightly. If you answer yes, then you will be asked why you want to undertake the process.

You may be aware of the hardness of the oak seat beneath you. You will hear the chirping sparrows in the ivy that partially covers the leaded windows of the room. You may notice the peculiar silver light of an early autumn afternoon that wants to fill the room. Will you notice the ticking clock atop the oak roll top desk? Are you aware that those seconds are precious, that they measure not only time but your life, and what you do with your body, your actions, your words, and your thoughts? You might look at the bone-handle magnifying glass resting on a pile of papers, and be fascinated by the silver reflection and the curved eye that stares at the ceiling. You do not have long to consider the question you have been asked. The heart knows what it knows, and you must speak from the heart.

Were you not expecting the question? You may not have a ready answer. That is fine. You should be aware that answers can be complex. You will be permitted to explain just how complex it is. You may tell a story to describe what you feel at the core of your answer. Stories are fine. Most people come to the first answer by way of experience. Something has touched them or spoken to them. Most people have a reason for coming to be asked the questions.

If you answer yes, the man seated opposite to you will say a silent prayer to himself. He will be pleased. You must understand that there is no easy road here. Your answer, if it is positive and thoughtful, suggests that there is some larger presence involved in your decision.

Do you have a story? If yes, you will be asked to tell it. You do.

꙳ You were walking along a small street in a prairie town late one hot afternoon when you met your first questioner. He was wearing a white, open-collar shirt. You have just come from the edge of the town where you leaned on the fence and looked into the distance where the flat fields and the enormous sky made you feel very small and lost in the way you tried to touch something other than the fence post and its wire. When you tried, you could not. You could see a city in the distance, but it seemed as near as the town's graveyard you walked to last evening thinking it was far away. You learned very quickly that there is no perspective on the prairie. Everything is near and everything is far at the same time.

You looked out the window of the residence where you were staying. Dinner would not be served for an hour, and you saw the trees you thought were at least a mile away. Someone said the town's burial grounds were out of town, and you took that to mean they were far out of town. To kill some time, you decided to walk there by yourself. You were curious about what it would be like to stand in the middle of nowhere and everywhere all at once. You had stared at the prairie during the previous days as the sun was setting and the evening gatherings were not yet ready to take place.

The silence intrigued you. So, did the space. It reminded you of being at sea, especially at night as you were driven from the airport to the college, and the lights on the horizon reminded you of passing ships in the night. You had seen the beautiful seabirds, the plovers and sandpipers, that hover over the stalks of wheat, especially after a mid-afternoon thunderstorm when the air is heavy, and hot, and you can hardly draw a breath.

When you reached the graveyard to visit the resting place of the founder of the small college, you were surprised the burial grounds had only been a two-minute walk from the dormitory. The trees had seemed much larger from far away. They were as tall as you. You heard crickets in the dry grass around the headstones. You paused for a moment at the resting place of the man who had founded the college, and you bent down and picked a piece of wild sage from the ground, held it to your nostril to inhale its incense of herb and sky, and placed it on his headstone. You felt a tremendous sense of peace as you stood there, but also a sense of loneliness, as if someone was standing beside you the whole time and followed you back to the town. You had the better part of an hour on your hands so you decided to explore the town. That is when you saw your first questioner. It was you who asked the questions then, wasn't it?

You'd met the man in the open collared white shirt during a Scrabble game the night before. He was a master of words. Even as you sat there with spare letters in your hand, you knew, as you looked at him, that he had something to teach you. When you saw him on the dusty side street, as devils in the hot afternoon wind danced around your ankles, you made a choice, a choice that would lead you to the moment of questions in search of a new name.

You walked up to the man in the open-collar shirt and asked him what you had to learn in order to be given your new name.

"You are considering this seriously?" he asked you.

"Yes." That is what brought you here, isn't it?

Are you ready for more questions now, more questions than you can possibly answer? Did you know that you have entered into a process of questions? It is not a game. It is not merely a matter of spelling something out. You will have to find answers. Perhaps another day. Go home. Think about it. Give your brain time to set the matter in order. You have a great deal to learn.

You thought about it for many months.

Did you notice during those months how life changed for you?

Can you remember the particulars of those changes?

Why have you decided that this moment, the early autumn afternoon, is the time when you will try to give your first answer?

You might be afraid that any answers you give are insufficient. That is a good sign. If you knew all the answers, there would be no reason to ask any questions.

You will return the following week to the office with the hard oak chair, the roll-top desk, and the leaded window. It will be raining the next time you arrive, and you balance your umbrella beside the coat stand, and sit down opposite your questioner in the hard, oak chair.

Do you believe there is an order to the world? he will ask you.

You will pause for a moment to consider.

In some ways, the world is a disordered place. The world is full of bad news. You have heard stories of suffering and despair on a daily basis because that is what informs you. But there is something else that informs you. Something you want to talk about but cannot know for sure. You might feel it deep inside you, but you do not know how to give it words.

If you answer yes, you will be asked if you believe there is a heart and a mind behind that order. Is there?

He is not talking about a heart and mind of flesh, but of something else. You could answer yes, but you might want to qualify the answer with an element of certainty. That is fine. Uncertainty is what the questions are leading to. If you are certain, you might be taken for a fool. If you are too certain, you might be mistaken for someone who has not asked enough questions of himself. If you are un-certain—and how uncertain are you?—what creates that uncertainty?

Your questioner will realize that you are caught be-tween knowing and not-knowing. That is a good thing. He will ask you, if you cannot be certain, if you are able to take something on belief?

Can you merely believe something or do you always have to know something? What is the difference?

Are you able to believe?

If so, what do you believe?

You believe many things. The world has constantly changed for you, and it is hard to believe just one thing.

You might remember the day when you felt very alone. You asked yourself this same question. You tell him you have been through a kind of living hell. You felt dead inside. In retrospect, you realize what you felt is different from the death inside you confronted when you stepped into the small dark box.

There are many kinds of death. Some are good, some are bad. Irreversible death is the one where you do not ask questions of yourself. You must try to remember this. Someone may ask you this on the day of your physical death, and you must prepare yourself to make an answer.

You had just left a bad job. Your former employer had been abusive to you. She had kicked you under the desk. She had said things such as: "You are not man enough to do this job." You had been demeaned and ridiculed in front of your fellow employees. She had constantly threatened to fire you. You were "worthless," she said in front of everyone.

One night you lashed out at her. You argued. You told her you weren't going to take it anymore. The snow was falling as you picked up your rolodex and walked into the night. The sidewalks were filling up with snow. The office buildings were empty, and the windows were darkened. The streetlamps lit up the sky with a yellow glow and every flake that fell was not white but the colour of fear. You had struggled to find a solution to a problem that could not be solved. Your boss had bared her lower teeth at you in anger because you could not solve the problem. Her anger reminded you of the ferocity of winter.

You had a dream one night. You thought, at first, it

was a nightmare. You were in Hell—or were you merely back in your office? There was a mathematical equation written on a dark, grey stone wall. You were told that everything depended on whether you could solve the problem. You would have perished in that dream. Dreams can kill a person. That is when something spoke to you in the dream.

What was it the voice said? Can you remember? Yes, you can. You know what the voice said. The voice said: "Do not attempt to answer the question. The question is Hell. The process of solving the question is Purgatory." That is when you woke. Your heart was pounding. Your wife was asleep beside you. You felt as if you were alone and abandoned in a dark place. Is that the same place you will find in yourself when you enter that small dark box? Think of this when you are in there, when you are alone with yourself and seeking the answers to the questions the voice will ask you.

Hell is the question. Purgatory is the process of finding the solution. What is the answer to the question on the wall? Figure it out. It isn't hard. You know the answer. It will come to you. It will be the first breath of wind in your sails as you embark on your journey. The answer contains the destination of the voyage you will undertake when you have a new name. You did not solve the problem. You refused. The question was just a decoy. You knew the answer. You accepted the answer because it was the only possible solution.

When did the solution come to you? Was it one night when you were still working late into the next day? A light in an office of a building directly opposite yours was burning late. It was two a.m. You were bent over a column of figures that would not add up. Your computer froze as if it had touched the pattern of frost on the window. The fluorescent light above your head was buzzing and you hadn't heard it until that moment when you felt so alone. You screamed to yourself, calling out a name that you thought might come to your assistance. The light buzzed as if it was blotting out every sound. You looked across the way. A woman was working at her desk. You stared at her as if to say: "You, too?" When she noticed you staring at her, she shut her blinds.

You were alone. You felt as if you had been reduced to nothing.

But there was something, there, wasn't there? It was the same presence you felt when you walked out to the graveyard outside that prairie town and realized that death, that end you had always felt was so far away, so remote, was closer than you could have imagined. You wanted something inside you to live forever, something that had always been a part of you even though you couldn't name it. You wanted something of what you were, and are, and will be, to remain always.

You tried to explain this to the man seated opposite you in the office while the autumn rain fell outside the window and the bright leaves of the maple tree spiralled to the ground. He nodded. Does he understand what you are saying, or are you merely babbling? He will tell you that you were in a bad situation, but that there is good in the world if you are prepared to open yourself to it.

Are you willing to admit that good is stronger than evil?

Do you love others as much as you love yourself? he will ask. Do you love others more than you love yourself?

You went home after the final shouting match with your boss. The snow fell and your life came apart. You knew that if you went back to work the next day you would be fired, that you would be reduced to nothing from who you were. You knew that others around you would also be fired—your secretary, your assistants, and your associates. Their lives, not just yours, depended on you finding the answer to the question that had been written on the wall of Hell.

You knew that everything you had accomplished, everything you had fought for and tried to do, everything that you thought was good, would lie in ruins around your feet if you went back into the hell of your office. If you went back, their lives would be ruined. If you stayed away, they might have a chance to redeem themselves, to be transferred to do something else. Their lives would not come apart.

You went home. Your wife and child were waiting for you. They were smiling. They were glad you had gotten out of a bad situation.

Did you know where you would go from there?

Did you know that an entire journey might unfold if you asked yourself what you really believed?

So, what do you really believe?

What are the things you hold most dear?

The man in the chair asks you more questions. That is his job.

Are you ready to explain what you carry with you, what you keep close to your heart, what you know?

Are you aware that all those things that are intangible cannot be taken from you?

Are you aware that your true value has no weight, no commercial worth, and no marketable exchange?

You tell the man in the chair about the silence. You sat one morning, quietly, in the house you feared you would lose because you no longer had a job and a paycheque. You only had what you carried inside you. And you asked yourself the question that is before you now. It is the question that set you on the process of finding your new name, of becoming your new self. You asked yourself: "What do I believe?" So, what do you believe?

You will realize the importance of that first question. It always has to be: "What do you believe?" You will find it on the opening page of the book the man seated opposite gives you. The book is long. There is so much to believe. You flip through it. Is belief an unsolvable question you will ask as you turn the pages? There is too much to believe. Far too much.

You scan the pages as you ride the subway home. You see how the book tries to explain the relationship between you and the universe. You are very small. The universe is very large. You realize just how easy it is to lose yourself in the great state of things. "You must understand," the man seated opposite you said as you put on your coat and picked up your umbrella, "that you save yourself by losing yourself."

If you say, "so be it," you are on your way. The process will be easy. You will find yourself waiting at the end of it.

Winter was a season of questions. You struggled with every answer. The man seated opposite you each week could not stop asking you questions. It was his job. He cares about the answers. He asks you more questions every time you answer. Eventually, you reached a point where the questions become redundant. There is only so much a person can know. There are limits. If he says you are ready, then you will proceed with him to the naming place.

You will enter the place of naming on a warm, spring afternoon. The blossoms will be opening in the garden. Lilacs. Forsythia. Hyacinths. There will be a perfume in the air. You will feel as if you have passed through death: the death of the world; the death you met within yourself in the small dark box where the voice asked you questions; the death of your old self. You will know that something has changed. You will breathe in a new way and you will not even notice it.

Your friends will say you are crazy for having sought a new name, that naming and renaming is old-fashioned, if not dangerous, and that a person doesn't need a name at all to live. You pay them no heed. Those who love you and support you will be there. They will have their doubts about what you are doing. They may whisper: "This is not right." But they will stand beside you as you as you take your new name and put on a new set of clothes. They are the clothes of a traveler. You will leave the place of naming. The sun will be warm on your face. You will have a sense that you know the way now, though no one will tell you how the journey will unfold or where it will take you. You will think of this day for the rest of your life because it brings a burden of uncertainty. You really don't know the way ahead. Take it one day at a time.

The man who was seated opposite you all winter will ask what name you have chosen. He will ask you what you believe.

Do you believe?

If you say yes, not merely to what you believe but that you have decided on a new name, he will bless you and call you by that name. You will have to choose your name carefully because it is not merely a name, but a purpose you undertake, a course you determine to sail.

If you say yes, you will find your way. Your new name is not merely who you are, but what you will become.

As you leave the naming place and step outside into the afternoon light, your eyes will take time to adjust. After a few minutes as your sight grows used to the change, everything will take on a different appearance. You will see where the path begins.

Elsie

Sealtest trucks were yellow and blue. Neilson trucks were red and white, and had a soldier made of circles and triangles painted next to the company name. His favourite, however, was the Borden truck. Borden's milk arrived in a white and yellow truck, and bore not only the name of the dairy but the image of Elsie. Elsie was a cow. Her smiling head poked through a wreath of yellow daisies with brown-eyed centres, and her silver-grey bell hung over the edge of the flowers.

Each day the milk trucks would roll up and down the street in front of Mervin's house. The milkmen in their blue or grey uniforms, bow ties, and peaked caps, always moved with a military precision up and down the driveways and front steps. They carried wire baskets that contained six bottles of milk, and sometimes they had small boxes of butter tucked under their arms. The Borden man always stopped on the porch and peered into Mervin's play pen. Mervin's mother parked him outside during the warmer months so he would grow strong in the fresh air. The Borden man always smiled, winked, and said: "Hi ya guy." Mervin looked forward to the Borden man. Mervin also looked forward to when his father came home at night, but instead of stopping to say hello to him, his father would brush by, face greasy with exhaustion, his clothes smelling of cigarette smoke, and say nothing. The Borden man was much nicer.

The supposition that ran through Mervin's mind was that each dairy had its own flavour of milk. His mother had screwed up her face when she mentioned Sealtest. "I don't like the taste of their milk," she had said as she shook her head.

The glass bottles had tin-foil caps, and round cardboard stoppers beneath the foil hats that Mervin played with when his mother opened a new quart. The bottles jingled with every step the milkmen took.

Mervin noticed that the neighbours were getting brown milk for their brood of boys who were always screaming and fighting in their front yard.

"Brown milk comes from brown cows," Mervin's mother said, and he took her word for it. "We drink white milk because it is healthier. And besides, brown milk makes those boys next door run wild."

The milkmen, themselves, were all different as well. The Sealtest man was short and dark-haired. His bow tie was always askance. He was round-shaped, and his face was sweaty. The Neilson's man wore some medals on his chest and was old. He had been a soldier in a war more than forty years before, and Mervin's mother remarked: "Poor guy, he's getting on."

Mervin called to the Neilson's man "hey poor guy," but that milkman never responded to his calls.

The Borden man was tall, and red-haired, thin, with black and gold frame glasses perched on his nose. He had a spring in his step. By noon of every morning when it was time for Mervin to come in and have his lunch and his nap, the parade of milkmen would have come and gone, leaving their jangling white and brown bottles on people's steps, or in boxes set into the walls at the side of each house. On hot days Mervin would catch the smell of something sour and unpleasant from the trucks, mostly the Sealtest truck. He imagined their milk tasted the way it smelled.

During the first summer Mervin remembered, his mother took him to the Exhibition. The swan rides were for girls. He watched the girls clamber aboard the large, hollow birds and announce to everyone that they were princesses. Mervin drove a shiny the blue car that went round and round the track, and made a beeping sound when he pressed the centre of the steering wheel. The girls in the swan looked over their shoulder and stuck out their tongues at him every time he beeped his horn.

A man snapped a picture of Mervin sitting inside a blue *Toronto Star* newspaper box, the kind he'd seen at each corner next to the red *Toronto Telegram* box and the orange and black *Globe and Mail* box.

Everything in the world had a name because it belonged to a company. His mother had said so. Gas stations, milk, eggs, groceries, dry cleaning, and newspapers such as the one his father sat behind each evening shaking his head "no" when Mervin asked him to play with him, all had names because they belonged to a company. When his mother announced that company was coming over,

Mervin was disappointed that they did not have names on the front of their clothes. His father held up a company name on his copy of the *Globe and Mail* every night and said very little.

By mid-afternoon of the day they went to the Ex, Mervin's mother had pushed his stroller through the crowds of people around the "Grand Stand," with its name "Stoodleigh" written on the wall.

"We're coming back here this evening so you can see the Musical Ride," his mother said as she bent down to wipe the piece of candy cotton off his hands. "You will love the Mounties." The Grand Stand cast a shadow over them, and Mervin grew tired and fell asleep. His mother woke him with her hand on his shoulder.

"Mervin! Mervin! You need to see this. You need to see Elsie!"

Mervin opened his eyes. Behind a wooden yellow fence, a golden brown and white cow lay on a bed of straw.

"Do you see? She is chewing her cud! Isn't that wonderful? That's Elsie!"

Mervin was confused. Where was her bell? Where was the ring of flowers? That was not Elsie. Elsie always smiled. A few minutes later his mother had wheeled him in front of a likeness of two men.

"That's Dwight Eisenhower and John Diefenbaker shaking hands. That one is the President of the United States, and the other is the Prime Minister of Canada where you live. They are the men who run the world," she marvelled and pointed to the figures. Mervin did not understand. The men were made of butter. Then he realized that butter, as well as milk, came to the door each day with the Borden man. The Borden man made the men who ran the world.

At the Grand Stand, Mervin fell asleep during a song sung by Milton Berle about what a problem kids were. He did not laugh at the jokes. He did not know what was funny about Milton Berle. Everyone else thought he was funny. Mervin felt confused and tired and closed his eyes.

Just for a moment much later, he opened his eyes. His mother was calling out to him: "See you haven't missed the Mounties!" as a man in a red jacket and a Smokey the Bear hat rode past slowly on a shiny black horse. The horse's haunches were glistening in the lights of the midway. Fireworks were exploding over the tower where a big yellow scallop shell, lit against the night, fanned out like flowers high above him.

He wasn't sure who was carrying him. The arms around him were strong yet gentle at the same time. His mother was walking behind, pushing his empty stroller, and he closed his eyes and went back to sleep.

Whenever Mervin thought about his life, it seemed a dream, even when he was a child. It was a boat floating merrily down the stream just like in the song.

There was one dream he had dreamed when he was sick. The doctor sat beside his bed. His mother was trying to hold back tears. The Borden man was there, too. The Borden man knelt beside Mervin's bed and said: "I'm so sorry buddy, I really am. In a way this is my fault." Mervin shut his eyes and went back to sleep. After that the Borden man never came to the house.

The Sealtest and Neilson trucks stopped coming to the neighbours. The last time Mervin saw a milk truck was one day when he was late heading back to school after lunch to his grade three class. The red, white, and blue Caulfield truck, a brand of milk few people used, rounded the corner at high speed and almost tipped over. The milk bottles inside clanged. That was the day the milk trucks disappeared. The truck must have been late for its own demise.

Mervin's father continued to pay little or no attention to him, and when he was home, Mervin seldom saw his father's face emerge from behind his daily news. At gatherings of his father's larger family, the boy stood out. He was different. His father's brothers and sisters and their children were all short and tanned. Their hair was stringy. Mervin was growing tall very fast, and his thick red hair made him different from the cousins.

"You look like the milkman," one of the girl cousins said in a taunt. His aunt hit her over the head with the flat of her palm. The girl turned on her mother. "Well, its true, you said so!" and got another slap.

Towering above one's family in height, being the only one to have a lean build, red hair, and glasses, bothered Mervin, though even into his teens he could not explain why. He and his father had grown even more distant and distrustful of each other. A prairie of silence fell between them and made dinners into icy affairs where questions were answered with either a "yes," but more often a grunting "no."

His mother said: "You should get to know your father." But Mervin always shrugged and said: "I don't know how."

The dreams Mervin had been having were puzzling to him. The more he dreamed, the more life bothered him.

He dreamed that the old black and white television in his parents' first house was on fire. The Borden man rushed in to haul the burning television set out of the living room and onto the front lawn. Mervin was watching from his play pen. The Borden man bent down with a screwdriver and took the back off the set, and swooshed away the smoke with his hand. The milkman reached inside the television and pulled out a stack of photographs. Elsie was standing beside the Borden man in her garland of yellow flowers. She was dancing with delight. There was nothing good on the television after nine a.m. when Captain Kangaroo signed off. The Captain joined the dance with Elsie. The boys next door came after them with sticks, and chased the cow and the Captain away. They turned on Mervin. The Borden man intervened, and took a giant crayon, and coloured them orange until they disappeared. Then the Borden man coloured himself orange, and cried, and disappeared, and Mervin woke up.

Mervin's mother was making dinner. Mervin's father was away again on a business trip, as he had always been when he wasn't around and Mervin was young. Mervin sat at the kitchen table, and looked up from his books. He was studying philosophy and was ploughing through Plato's *Republic*. Plato seemed to have the right idea. A child, almost at birth, was taken away from his parents and raised with the idea that the state was his identity. A person in the republic didn't have to worry about whether he was different from his family.

"Was I adopted?" he asked.

His mother turned to him. "No! What would give you that idea?"

"I don't look like any of the others in Dad's family."

"You take after my side."

"So your five-foot-six family, and Dad's five-foot-four family, had the genes to make me six-three? And what about the hair?"

"Someone somewhere back when looked just like you, I'm sure of it."

"I keep having these strange memories. The Borden man." His mother put down her paring knife, and rolled her eyes.

"You remember him?"

"Was I very ill when I was about four?"

"You almost died. Gastroenteritis. There was a huge outbreak of it all over the city mostly up around where we were living. About eighty children were hospitalized. We took you to the hospital, but they didn't have a bed so we brought you home. They told us you were going to die. The doctor sat up with you all night. You got better. About twenty children didn't."

"What caused it?"

"Borden's milk. A truck that went around the north end where we lived lost its refrigeration, and the driver was in a hurry to get his route done for the day, so he delivered the milk. The papers blamed him, but the truth was that the dairy equipment hadn't been cleaned properly."

"That's when we stopped home delivery?"

"That's when I started doing a weekly shopping in the store. We stopped getting bread to the house. Your grandmother found a cigarette butt in a loaf, and that was the end of that for her and me."

"Mail used to come in red trucks, didn't it."

"You remember the trucks? The streets were a parade of trucks. The Royal Mail, the milkmen, the cleaners, the bakeries, Eaton's, Simpsons. The lady across the road even had her eggs delivered in a white truck, and her fruit in a yellow truck ..."

"With a cornucopia of grapes and bananas spilling over the writing."

"You have some memory."

"So, Mom, when I was sick, did the Borden man come to see me in my room?"

His mother looked at him, and Mervin saw anger in her eyes.

"At the time we thought he had made you and the other children ill. I wouldn't have let him across the threshold. Everyone said he was a murderer."

"Did the television catch fire?"

"What's bringing on this walk down memory lane?"

"I'm just curious. I've been having flash-back dreams, and I'm trying to sort out what happened and what didn't happen."

"Yes. You played postman one day when I wasn't keeping an eye on you, and you mailed photographs, mostly your early childhood pictures, into the slots on the side of the set. I turned on my soap operas one afternoon when you were having a nap, and the firemen came after the cleaner's delivery man hauled the set onto the front lawn. I got you up just in time to see the fire reels drive off. You were very disappointed. You loved firemen."

"What became of the Borden man?"

"How should I know? He was a delivery man."

"He used to speak to me when he came to the house. I remember that."

"You spoke to everyone. The doctors said that you needed to be outside to get fresh air, so when you were a baby I put your carriage on the porch, and later your play pen. You'd sit there for hours and holler at everyone who came and went."

"He had red hair, didn't he? The Borden man."

"Your great-grandfathers had red hair. You look like them. You couldn't miss with it being on both sides of the family. And tall, too." She went back to chopping her carrots, and life kept pushing Mervin through days and names to the point where he started to forget more than he remembered.

When Mervin's son and daughter were born they each bore a striking resemblance to Mervin's father who, in his declining years in poor health filled out in his face, his head bald, and his cheeks dimpled. Mervin fell asleep with his four-week-old daughter nuzzled on his chest. Her fist curled around a bunching in his sweater, and with the warmth of the baby upon him, his sleep became deeper than anything he had ever known.

He found himself in the middle of a field of yellow flowers with brown centres, and as he moved through the field, he came upon Elsie who was seated, a garland around her neck, and a silver cow bell dangling over the petals. As the flowers blew in the wind, he thought he heard the jingling of milk bottles rattling against each other. The clouds were milk-white and the sky was bright blue.

"Nice to see you again," she said to Mervin. "I didn't think you'd ever return."

"Why have you been in my life?" he asked.

"I'm your holy cow. Everyone has a holy cow of some sort. They see something surprising and they call out my name so I can help them figure it out."

"What do holy cows do other than sit in fields or show up at the Ex?"

"We answer questions. Fire away. I know you have some."

"Okay. I need to know this one. Was the Borden man my father?"

"Nasty cousins, eh? I warned that little bitch not to say that to you. I even made her choke on her milk one day when she was giggling and started to blow it out her nose."

Elsie shook her head and paused for a moment, looking around the field of yellow flowers as if they contained the answer.

"Mervin, Mervin, you've spent your whole life in doubt. You've never been able to talk to your father because, deep down inside, you thought that red-haired milkman was your father. I'm sorry to say that he wasn't. The milkman, that is. Your father is your father. He spent his life either away earning a living so you could have a good life and get a good education, or exhausted behind a newspaper with nothing to say to you because he didn't have the energy. You were down near the ground. If you'd been standing up when he came home jack tired every night you would have seen the desperation in his eyes. He was as frightened of you as you were of him, and the two of you never really talked because neither of you knew what to say. He was a business man. You're a philosopher. The two rarely talk to each other except in questionable self-help books. And don't read those. They're written by people who didn't get enough milk as children."

Mervin woke with a start. His chest was burning, and the burning was spreading into his arm pits. He thought he was having a heart attack, but it was only his daughter whose diaper had leaked. She was fast asleep, just where he had laid her down upon him. She was smiling and the look on her face reminded him of his father.

When Mervin buried the man he had never really been able to talk to, he thought about the milkman who everyone said could have been his real father—the jovial delivery guy who brought quarts to the house that were so easily mistaken for the milk of human kindness. His real father, whom he saw so seldom that his face faded into memory even while he was still alive, had eyes he could not remember.

What colour were his father's eyes?

Had his face always been dimpled?

Had he been a strong man, strong enough to carry a hot, sleeping child through the Exhibition grounds after a long, hard day at work?

With the funeral proceedings over, the cemetery keepers resumed cutting the grass. A gas mower roared several rows beyond the open grave where his father's sarcophagus sat perched on three two-by-fours over the open earth. Behind the mower, a tall, hunched man pushed and tugged at the handles of a Toro. His hair was faded to a yellow white, not quite the colour of Elsie's flowers, but close to it. The man must have had red hair at some point in his life. Maybe that was him—the milkman who had saved him from the neighbourhood bullies, who had carried the burning television set onto the front lawn, who had always winked at Mervin as he sat in his play pen on the porch as he learned to read the names on delivery trucks.

Mervin waved, but the gardener simply shook his head as if, *go away, I have nothing to say*, and continued twisting and turning his machine between the headstones. Mervin stared at the open ground before him, and the mat of plastic Astroturf that covered the shovelling that would be returned to the soil.

The others had left to comfort Mervin's mother, and to stand around at the stiff afternoon tea and talk about the man Mervin had never really got to know. He picked a yellow flower from one of the wreaths that were to be thrown into the grave, laid it atop the sarcophagus, and continued the wordless conversation he always held with his father.

Mercury Row

i) *Verandas*

Mercury Row ran along the northern lakeshore as far as the paved road. It was the best part of the lake fifty years ago. A person could idle his outboard engine, even cut it, and drift past the cottages situated atop rock promontories. The smell of martinis and cigarette smoke wafted from the screened verandas as early as noon every day when summer cottagers on the row began to stir. The wealthy, who laid claim to shoreline on the best part of the lake, had names like Bob and Doris, Gladys and Frank—good solid names that meant they'd come by their money the way it should be come by—through inheritance—and that their grandparents, up from Toronto to play pioneer in the bush every summer for the few weeks the Exchange slowed down, had established something lasting and powerful.

The row got its name in the Sixties because there was a pecking order to the brand of motors a family used on their launch. Mercurys were the most expensive, and had the most horse-power. The housings of the engines glistened in chrome and had a smoother, more musical, running voice. A person could hear a Mercury coming, and that was the point of having one. Farther down the lake, where the shallows emptied into the river and the waters became murky and reedy, was a run of smaller, less well-kept cottages known as Evenrude with the *rude* punctuated for good effect when it was spoken. The Evenrudes were louder and fat-sounding, but were far more affordable. Motors on the lake were a matter of social distinction.

Arch was the main man on Mercury Row. Everyone, except those who lived down the lake in Evenrude, loved Arch for his quips and his financial savvy. To the less well-off, Arch was just one of the rich guys who had a cottage where the water deepened and the mosquitoes were fewer. He had a soft-top electric blue Caddy, and the kids from Mercury Row would drive up and down the logging roads with him at night and let the breeze run through their crew cuts and blond braids. Arch loved to stay out all day in his launch because that motor, that Mercury motor, had enough power to vroom him from one end of the lake to the other in under five minutes. He would take Frank and Bob and George fishing with him early on foggy mornings when the lake was glass, and if they sat with the motor off down in sight of Evenrude they'd usually come home with a catch that Doris or Gladys (but usually Marie) would clean for the evening meal. Life was good on Mercury Row until George complained of fatigue and dropped dead one evening as he sat on Frank's porch with his third martini in-hand and a Romeo y Julieta torpedo in the other, baked down to its decorative ring.

Marie, who was George's wife, was always the odd woman out among the crew because she was French Canadian, and a Catholic, who had permitted her children to attend private school in Toronto with the other boys from the row. By the time George keeled over, the kids on the row were grown, had jobs on the Exchange, and only had a week or two off to get up to the old stomping grounds.

Everything was sad for several weeks that summer. Frank said the fish weren't biting, and Arch kept having motor trouble. When Marie returned to Mercury Row, the other women, especially Gladys, felt sorry for her. There were extra offerings of noon-time martinis poured for Marie who lingered over them because she was not, by nature, a drinker and even less of a smoker. She didn't mind cleaning the catch of the day, and she was the first into the kitchen and usually the last one out when the gang gathered.

Arch convinced the girls that they should come along on the fishing expeditions, and though the lake was not large enough to go too far from the cottages, Gladys and Doris joined Arch and Bob in the boat for the early morning spin. Marie, who said she was very much in mourning for George, begged off. She had just returned to the cottage after dealing with her husband's estate in the city. She wasn't fond of boats. Frank also decided to stay behind to oversee the men from the main road who were coming to fix a problem with his cottage's roof. That was when it happened.

Frank stuck his head in Marie and George's place to see if she needed any handy work done, and that is when he saw her coming naked out the bedroom, confronting him with only a smile on in the middle of the living room. For a moment they looked at each other, embarrassed. Then Marie said: "Certainly you've seen a woman naked before." To which Frank replied that he had but he hadn't realized she was that good looking. Marie moved toward him and put her head on his shoulder and began to cry. At first, Frank didn't know what to do as her sobs deepened and she explained that George had been "distant" for many years and had probably been carrying on with a young man who lived just beyond the dump on the main road. "They met by moonlight," she whimpered.

An hour later, Frank got up and dressed. He heard the gang coming back down the lake and the laughter from the boat. He rummaged around in one of the lower kitchen drawers, found George's hammer, and emerged from the cottage carrying the ballpeen in case any of the gang saw him leaving. By the next summer, as the cottages on Mercury Row were re-opened for the season and the noon-time scent of cigarettes and martinis mixed with the natural scent of pine and the sturdy base aroma of stone, lake water, and outboard exhaust, Marie had a new child, a boy.

Gladys and Doris sat together on Doris' screened porch and discussed the math. The child was how old? Hadn't George been dead how long? And hadn't Marie confessed to them, one afternoon shortly after George's passing, that he'd been distant? The kid had to be a bastard. Gladys had seen George with the Willows boy who lived on the main drag. Who could the father be, they wondered? And just as they remembered that Frank and Marie had been left alone that day when Arch and Bob took them off to a special fishing spot they'd discovered at the far end of the lake, the sound of a child crying, hungry after its morning nap, broke the stillness of Mercury Row.

"Damned kids," Doris said. "I thought we were all past that long ago. She's too old to be having a new one, and by God-knows-who."

"You don't need to ask God," Gladys replied. "I'm sure the kid has Frank's eyes."

"Are you going to do anything?" Doris said, leaning forward so her voice was hushed in almost a whisper.

"Damn right, I am. I'm buying that kid a canoe as soon as it can stand on two legs. I'll teach it to paddle. Someone else, whoever else, can teach it to swim if it has a mind to learn."

"And if it doesn't?"

"Let's hope it doesn't."

ii) *The Lure*

Dave Willows wanted to see Paris but the closest he got was a postcard tacked to the cigarette rack behind the counter at the Lure Shop that Lois had sent him. It was of the Eiffel Tower.

Lures were his primary business, but over the years, because the general store owned by his uncle had shut down prematurely in the late Forties just before the boom came along in the Fifties and Sixties, Dave had gone into tackle. His uncle had explained, sadly, that there wasn't much happening half the year except to sit there in the silence and wind thread around hooks and feathers to make Woolly Buggers for the tourists. Once Dave got his hands on the ramshackle store, he expanded the Lure into a trading post. He carried most of the daily essentials— milk (when it was fresh and the fridge worked), bread (when the truck came in), canned goods (lots of canned goods), and, of course, smokes.

In later years, he would strike it rich when he got a license from the LCBO to be a purveyor of spirits, and, after earning his certificate to provide scuba gear, he would give lessons and rent out tanks to the summer folks. There wasn't much to see at the bottom of the lake, and along the Evenrude shore a person could stand up to his knees on the muddy bottom. Dave put the story out that a prospector had lost his pouch of gold nuggets, and that made the teenagers shell out their money for gear rental. But Dave gave up any claim to being a scuba diver after he assisted the police in their search. He had been the one who made the discovery everyone feared would be made, and he said after that he wouldn't go back in the lake. He would never explain why to anyone, except when he wrote a letter to Lois—a letter he never sent—that he had seen something at the bottom of the lake and could not get the image out of his mind. As he aged along with his trading post and went from standing behind the counter to sitting out front in a battered station chair, the corners of his mouth turned down, and everyone who suspected what he might have known or thought, passed on or passed away. What he had seen was a secret he relegated to a footnote in a life he regretted living.

Dave saw it all pass by along the highway. The lake went from a derelict area to a reborn area as city types scrambled to snatch up waterfront property. They'd heard someone say that it wasn't being made anymore. That sent the values through the roof. The old cottagers of Mercury Row moved on, or died, or let their places fall to wrack and ruin, and the new cottagers had come in, torn down the old clapboard structures with their screened verandas and knotty pine panelling to build more sumptuous vacation homes on the shadows of the old ones. The lure business went on making less and less money. The bread and milk business did okay. Lois stopped writing, and the postcards' blues faded to a parchment colour until there was little left to see except a defiantly white border around an emptiness.

The postcard of Paris appeared several months after Lois had left him for her French adventure. Her first card arrived on a spring afternoon, just as things were returning to life on the main road and the ice had vanished from the shoreline. Lois had declared, as the first snow was falling the previous October, that she couldn't take another winter of silence with the only break in the soundlessness being between gasps of the wind howling around the corners of the trading post and the sound that trees make when they can't hold up the weight of snow on their boughs any more—a kind of cracking nature makes at its wit's end. She couldn't watch him sitting there winding, and gluing, and making Woolly Buggers night after night, especially when there weren't fish in the lake anymore that anyone had seen or caught. She asked him why he wasn't coming with her, why he was throwing away his God-given talent as a painter when he could go with her to Paris.

Dave had replied that he couldn't afford just to pick up stakes and leave, and besides when the cottagers returned there'd be plenty to do. She went to the side wall where he sold his paintings of rocks and trees, and of rocks, trees, lakes, and the odd motor boat with a Mercury strapped to the back—the Evenrude people never purchased paintings of their boats and Dave had learned not to paint what he didn't have a market for—and flung the one of Gladys and Frank's cottage at his head. The painting had been a commission, but after it was dry and Dave had even varnished it for posterity, they said it wasn't up to snuff and wouldn't even hang it in their guest bedroom. That hurt. If he'd painted Montmartre they might have bought it, she said.

"I just can't pick up and leave," he said, so she left.

She said she'd got a job working as a dancer, but didn't say where. He stopped himself from imagining her in a place like the Crazy Horse or the Folies Bergère, though he had a hunch she'd landed somewhere in Pigalle along with so many other girls from the north who had declared their love of Paris and gone off to find it. She could have become an *au pair*, but that would have unsettled her. She never liked children.

What unsettled Dave was the fact that he knew he had talent if only he could learn more. He'd started off as a kid with paint-by-numbers, but the damned kits never came with enough paint, at least not the way he liked to put it on. Some of the other kids did paint-by-numbers during the winters, but they never filled in all the spaces completely. One guy had the nerve to come in one day and ask Dave if he'd like to sell his old paint-by-numbers along with the fresh, freehand paintings, but Dave had said no and the guy refused to come back and did his shopping twenty miles away at another trading post on the main highway.

To increase his income, Dave had taken a correspondence course in small motor mechanics. He would use his spare cash to pick up old outboards, especially the discarded Johnsons, Deeres, and Evenrudes. The Mercury parts were harder to come by. He had to call a guy in North Bay for those, but eventually, as something better came out each year, the folks on Mercury Row would trade up for newer, faster models, and rather than have them lying around their domains in the undergrowth, they'd take them to Dave and he'd give them a few bucks for them for scrap.

By the time Lois left, there was a handsome pile of rusting Mercurys forty feet back of his shop in the pine scrub. Some had their covers missing and looked like pianos with the lids raised, while others just seemed to age during the winter, a little rust here and there until the paint wore off and the chrome spotted like a leopard. He'd found a spare part for Frank's motor one day and was delivering it when he heard the conversation that stayed with him and unnerved him for years.

Frank had managed to avoid oiling his motor and burned out a bearing one day in the middle of the lake. He had drifted until he could wave down one of the Evenruders who was attempting to teach his kid water-skiing, though everyone knew there wasn't enough power in the lower cottager's cheap hitch to get the kid up on his feet, let alone trail behind an aluminum dingy. The kid, still in his life jacket, grabbed Frank's tow rope and brought them back to shore. When Frank tied up at his dock, Dave looked at the motor as its tail rose out of the water and the cowling was off. "It kind of looks sad with its innards all hanging out," Dave had commented.

"Just fix the damn thing and let me know how much it will be. I don't want to sit around here all summer watching the grass needing to be cut."

When Dave returned with the right part it was noon-time a week later, and he found that Frank had gone somewhere with Bob, and the girls were all over at Marie's waiting for her to cook them lunch. He could smell Gladys and Doris' cigarettes and caught the scent of the day's first martinis being poured.

Gladys was talking to Marie's kid, the one who had appeared after George's death as a late-life afterthought. The boy was about seven, Dave reckoned. Gladys, by this time, had grown raspy from the smokes, and her voice reminded him of stones in a cement mixer, and the effect of the smokes on her throat had made her speak loudly to compensate for what she was losing in sound. Before knocking, Dave hung by the screen door at the forest side of the cottage.

"What do you call those knights, Pierre?"

"They aren't knights. They are cuirassiers."

Marie said: "I bought him several kits of Waterloo soldiers to paint while he was up here because there aren't any kids to play with his age."

"Did you know the French lost the Battle of Waterloo?" Doris, also in the living room while watching Marie cook, said.

Pierre must have looked up. "They were cavalry."

Dave heard a crunch as if someone had just stepped on something small and breakable, and then the boy cried and shouted for his mother.

"I'm sorry," Gladys said. "I didn't see your toy. Just get some glue. Besides, you shouldn't be playing with French soldiers. They're no good."

There was a silence and then Dave heard Marie say: "Get out." And Gladys and Doris left by the lakeside door off the screened veranda, the frame slapping shut behind them on its spring. The boy sobbed.

Dave decided he would catch up with Frank later. He never forgot the sound of that toy soldier snapping under what was probably Gladys' foot.

iii) *The Toast*

On a jut of land down the way from the newest place on Mercury Row sits a large building—a boathouse or a cottage. But it is the view from the picture window of a post and beam lodge that Rich recalls every time he has the dream. He is with two, perhaps three ladies. They are raising their glasses. Beyond the picture window, a stand of trees lines the far shore and, through the trees they are looking into, the setting sun seems to stop momentarily. That is when time stands still and the dream ends.

The dream has been coming to Rich since before the snow began to fall. It is March now. He thinks he slept through winter like a bear. He wonders where the lake is and who the women are. He gave up drinking several years ago when he started to dream the lives of people he had never known. In those dreams, he could not find a way out of a red and yellow basement with no windows or doors. This dream, the one he is having now, waking and sleeping—it never wants to go away—is different. There is a way out, but he has forgotten the way in.

Not being able to remember is a good thing, he has overheard his friends say when they thought he wasn't listening. He has told his doctor about the dream, and his doctor has also said it is a good thing. When the dream comes, Rich feels happy to relive the first weeks of spring where the dream always wants to begin. Rich knows he will have to understand what happens moments later, after the sun goes down, after the clink of glasses, and the first sips of wine. He knows that, but why interrupt a beautiful moment?

So, where was the lake? He wants to know. His friends are sitting at his kitchen table. It is as far from a lake as anyone can be in a country of lakes. They are drinking coffee. He has just told them again about the dream. They are silent. They stare into their mugs. Arlene looks up and tries to smile at Rich.

"You really don't remember, do you?" He asks her to tell him and she says: "Later." The friends nod. "There will be many laters," Arlene says.

Rich decides that when it comes again he will stay in the dream until the dream ends. The friends are sipping their wine. The sun has finally been pulled into the brown horizon of trees.

"Let's go down to the dock and watch the stars come out. There will be meteors tonight," one of the women says. Rich takes her hand. He feels she is more beautiful than anyone he has known. He cannot see her face and wants to see it more than anything else, but it is dark and the boughs of pines deepen the shadows.

The limestone slabs are cemented together, but Rich still must watch his footing because the afterglow is burning down like a kerosene lamp and he is carrying his glass of wine. There's Venus, he thinks. There's another light in the sky. He knows the name for it but cannot find the word. The dock should have been a better dock, but it shifts under everyone's feet. Rich lets go of the woman's hand and stands on the edge where an eye ring droops next to his left foot. He looks up.

For a moment, he feels he is falling but he holds on to his glass. He does not want to spill his wine. One of the women screams. A sudden blackness slaps at the back of his head.

When he wakes, he phones Arlene.

"What was I doing on the dock?"

Arlene is silent.

"Please tell me. Please."

"You are coming back now. Rich, you fell in the water and struck your head on a boulder."

"There was a woman whose hand I was holding. What was her name?"

"That was your wife. Her name was Martha."

"Was?"

"Rich, she jumped in to rescue you. The water shocked her and she had a heart attack and drowned."

The realization that Rich had lost Martha, the return of his memory, was hard enough to take. He understood, at last, what the void was that filled his life, the way a person lives with what is familiar and learns to see it and keeps seeing it until it is gone and someone else must point out it is no longer there. He feels he must mourn her. He knows now why the bedroom closet is partially empty. He knows why there were oil marks on the floor of the two-car garage and only one car, waiting to be driven again when he is well enough. His friends had done a thorough job removing traces of Martha. Maybe it was from kindness, but Rich feels a rage at what is missing. And he keeps having the dream.

He is falling off the dock in the twilight. The feeling of weightlessness catches hold of him and shakes him awake but he fights it until, in the dream, he is certain he is in the water. That is where he had seen something that truly frightened him, something more than the touch of his wife's hand on his wrist and the sudden, almost spasmodic tightening of her grasp. He can feel those things in his dream. But it is what he sees.

He is in the water, looking up at a dock, an old plank one with a worn tire tied to the side as a bumper for a motor boat. The sun is glistening and twisting everything out of shape. His eyes sting as he looks at the spattering of rays on the footings and the green bottom where the rocks nest in their water moss. Two women are talking, but he can't make out their words—not on the first hearing. The sun goes dark. A canoe is lowered on top of him. He wakes.

He tells Arlene during one of their late-night phone conversations that were more frequent as Rich grappled with the realization of Martha's loss: "There was something else in the lake, something that frightened me and I can't understand what it was."

"Try not to fixate on it, honey. You've lost the one person who meant more to you than anyone else, and that's enough of a blow. Maybe, deep down, something inside you is trying to explain what it was to have Martha beside you, fighting for you, while at the same time unable to fight for herself."

Maybe that was it, but the feeling that something else, perhaps someone else, was there beside him, tears at Rich.

"You know, honey, we were all in the lake, fishing you out first because we saw your head bleeding and then we went back in after Martha when she was motionless."

At last, Rich fought long enough to stay in the dream —the sunset, the toast, the path down to the dock, the fall off the dock, the feeling of something impacting on his head—then he saw what he knew was there.

A boy reached out for him. The boy had sad eyes, but his flesh was tight against his bones as if he had starved to death. The boy opened his mouth and tried to speak to him. He knew what the boy was saying. Sadness. His jaw tried to cry and all that poured out was sadness. Rich wanted to scream, but just as if he was trying to shout underwater, a scream in a dream is impossible. Was it a scream of pain? No, he did not think so. It was a scream of companionship, that was the only way to explain it. Companionship. They understood each other. He understood what the boy knew.

Two women are standing with the boy on his dock. Rich thinks, but isn't sure, that they are the women who once owned cottages where his post and beam place now stands. They are pointing to a new, green, fibreglass canoe. The boy feels tremendously happy. He looks up at his own cottage, the third in the row of four atop the rocky crest at the end of the road where the paving stops, and thinks he should ask his mother, but she is nowhere to be seen.

"Isn't this your son's new canoe?" the boy asks one of the women.

"He's spoiled. He bought it and then he says he doesn't want it, so it is yours. I'm giving it to you as a present. Go ahead. Try it out. Long, slow strokes. You'll love it. It will be fun. You'll be a *voyageur*, just like your ancestors. You will discover the north. You will fathom all the magic and mystery this place holds. You might find that missing gold out there somewhere. Dave Willows says it is the lake's treasure. You heard him say that at the trading post the other day. Maybe they'll name a bay after you when you find it."

The two women pick the canoe up by the bow and the stern and lay it in the water. One of them bends down to steady it as the boy steps in, pressing his shaking wrists on the gunwales as they hand the paddle to him. The canoe rocks beneath his weight and he struggles to balance it while holding on to the tire bumper.

"Careful. You don't want to tip. The balance will come," the woman says while the other is silent, staring at him, staring into him. "It is easy."

He kneels as if he is praying. They hand the boy the paddle. He places the paddle on the gunwales of the canoe, then raises it and dips it in the water.

"Go now," the woman who has been silent says. Her voice is raspy. "Go now. Eternal mysteries are waiting for you out there in the lake."

He dips his paddle in the water, and tiny drops fall from each stroke.

The Good Old Days

I was standing in the corner with a drink in my hand. I had just finished a discussion about a current project that was nearing completion when across the room I saw a woman who looked very familiar. She was tall, elegant, with brown hair in a page-boy, and a freckled complexion. I nodded and she nodded back.

We approached through the crowd and spoke. "How have you been?" she asked.

"Busy lately." Then, and I don't know why, I added: "Do you do much travelling these days?"

She looked puzzled and cocked her head to one side. "No," she replied with hesitation. "I'm on a school teacher's salary at a local girl's academy and I rarely have enough left over to do much."

"But you always had money, didn't you?"

"No." She started sizing me up and I read in her face the same look of disconnection that she must have seen in mine.

"But just now, I pictured you in my mind. You were standing beside a fountain in Italy ... I'm not sure which fountain, but it is in a square. Your hair is slightly different —you still have the same page-boy cut, but I seem to recollect that I saw you wearing a large sun hat with a turquoise ribbon through the brim and the bow tied under your chin."

"I'm beginning to think we've never met. I've never been to Italy. You're mistaking me for someone else."

I apologized and we bantered about writing for a few minutes before someone grabbed my elbow. I offered to look at her short stories and give her some suggestions —the reflected wisdom of a literary scholar. On my way home I could not get over the very unsettling feeling that comes when I've run into people who I feel, deep down, that I know and have known well. It happened several times in the past few months. A colleague's husband and I almost shut down a party because we both knew that we had been to the same place, though we couldn't name it or say where, and we knew small details about each other. I got his telephone number and told him we would sort it out. As he was leaving, he turned to me. "Do you still have a black border collie?"

"I do!"

"She never leaves your side, does she? She's always there."

At home after that peculiar gathering, I sat on the couch with my dog beside me. The old wisdom goes that one does not choose the dog, the dog chooses you. I buy that. Dogs have instincts and they read people better than we read ourselves. I put my head back and closed my eyes. The dog curled up next to me. I was not sure what it was I should be remembering.

The old dream that keeps coming back visits me again. I am walking along a hillside road. I look over the valley below and on the other side is a stone cottage with two gables poking from the slate roof. As the road ahead of me climbs, I see a man leaning on his wooden rake ... or is it a scythe? He is wearing a white shirt and a black vest and dark, baggy pants. He is cutting the chaff and weeds from the roadside. He takes off his pork-pie cap to mop is brow. He has white hair. The dog and I approach him.

"When will you be going?" he always asks.

"Soon," I say. "Any day now." I bend down to pat the dog that has come out of the brush to nuzzle my legs. I am wearing khaki jodhpurs and tall brown riding boots. My shirt sleeve is a blue and white stripe, and I notice where the tops of my braces fasten into the trousers.

As usual, something wakes me at that point. The dog stirs and growls out the window. Every time the dream visits me I try to go back, try to see what happens next, but I am pulled by the world of my conscious reality, by my responsibilities and obligations here. But I think about the man. I know him. He is my colleague's husband who shares the sense that we have known each other somewhere. My right shoulder aches as I think about the man's face. I have known him all my life.

I telephone my cousin who is an experimental psychologist. She loves to dabble in dreams and dream therapy. She tells me my recurring dream could be a past life experience. "Are you hiding something?" she asks. "Have any unfinished business from long ago?"

"I don't know. It was not my business, at least not as I know my business now."

"You should consider having a past life regression."

"Why?" I say. "I'm regressive enough in this life." But the thought of finding out what is hiding inside me is a powerful temptation. I can't keep my mind off the khaki jodhpurs and the brown riding boots. They were officers' standard dress during the First World War.

As a young boy my parents took me to meet the Prime Minister in Ottawa. He signed my autograph book in the House of Commons. Afterwards, they took me to the War Museum. There was a replica dugout set up there so that visitors could understand what the war had been like. The floors, however, were neatly swept concrete and the room with its eerie blue half light glowing as if just past sunset over No-Man's Land was punctuated by a Lewis gun propped above the parapet. I stood there transfixed. I hated the place yet did not want to leave. I felt I couldn't. My mother came looking for me.

"We've been all over the place. Have you been here the entire time? You're missing Brock's tunic and sash."

"The damn gun is jammed," I retorted in a harsh tone. "I can't change the canister." I wrestled with the gun. "Who disabled this? Who? Who!" She grabbed my arm and dragged me out. That is when the dream started chasing me.

The woman I met at the party, the woman I felt I had known somewhere, emailed me some of her writing. She had written a story about a young woman in Rome. She and her new husband were on their honeymoon. The brilliant sunlight and the gentle heat of an Italian spring seemed to last forever, and they stood beside the decorated fountain and clutched each other's arms as pigeons circled above them sounding the flutter of angels' wings. "Make it last forever," the character said to her smiling spouse. "Make it last forever."

I emailed her with some suggestions once I had read the manuscript. "I thought you said you had never been to Italy," I noted in my email.

She wrote back to me: "I haven't. I was writing about a dream I keep having."

"And the husband in the dream, the one in the tweed suit and the Panama hat … what era is that set in?" I knew it was Edwardian. She did not respond to my message for several days.

"I am sorry for not replying sooner, but I've had the dream again and I saw the man more carefully this time. He had your face."

Her email was unsettling, and I was uneasy answering it until I woke the next morning. My dream had come again, but this time it was much longer.

The scene of the man on the road is only the middle of the larger story that visits me. A woman with dark, short hair cut in a page-boy is standing beside me at the altar of a small country church. She reaches out for my hand. I re-move a pair of brown gloves and place them inside my officer's cap that another man is holding though I cannot see his face. And as I take her hands in mine, I look up and through the veil I see her—the face and eyes of the woman from the party. As we leave the church and people are standing around us, cajoling and laughing, I whisper to her: "Time is so short." Tears well up in her eyes. I lean close and kiss her and the gathered friends cheer in unison.

The room with the heavy comforter on the bed is

warmed by a small fire. There are birds singing in the eaves or far out on the grassy hillsides, and when I rise to look out the window, I see a landscape stripped of its trees, the mountains rising and falling in the distance as if the whole world is alive and breathing. And I hear the breathing of someone in the room with me, and it is her. The coverlet has slipped from her shoulders and I look on the moment with wonder that moves me to the core of my being. I think: "I shall take this with me to the end."

I am suddenly flooded by images I do not understand, but I know them from her stories. She has a better memory of that part of the dream than I. Then the road appears again. I am with the dog that will not leave my side. I pass through the dugout of the War Museum.

There are shouts I cannot decipher and pangs of exhaustion. I am sitting on a wooden firing step. My breath is curling as if a cloud in front of me. There is a young man beside me. His eyes are grey, and wide, and innocent, and he is shivering. He whispers: "I'm so cold, Lieutenant. What I wouldn't give for a bowl of me Mom's soup." I pat him on the knee. "I know what a warm hearth would do for me right now, and a warm bed, and my warm wife." The air is incredibly still. The world is incredibly quiet and calm. Inside I feel as if I have nothing to fear any longer.

"Sir," says the young man who has mud speckled among his freckles, "will it always be like this? Do you think that we've missed out on life and are just here forever?"

"No. It will pass. Just think of the good old days. There'll be more of those." And suddenly, it all goes black. I have not lost the dream. The dream and I are still joined. I feel as if I am flying but I am not sure which way is up. The young man is in front of me and before I can grab him to hold me down, he passes through me, through my right shoulder, and we thud back down to earth and the earth thuds on top, drowning us. And I see the stone cottage again, and the hillside road, and the dog walking up and down the road as if the pup is searching for something, and comes to greet me. She sits in front of me and turns her head, as if puzzled, as if trying to figure an answer to something I have asked and she cannot fathom.

When I woke, I immediately thought that I had to do something for the three of us. I telephoned the school teacher. "I had the dream again. I read your stories. This is going to sound incredibly strange, but there is someone you have to meet. And we need to talk."

I phoned my colleague's husband. He had been having dreams about a young woman who he had failed terribly. "I know where we can have lunch. Can you? There is someone I am going to bring along and you need to meet her." We all agreed to gather in a late-day breakfast place on Bloor.

I arrived first, then the teacher, and then the colleague's husband. Once we had taken off our coats and blown into our hands to warm them against the winter midday, we stared at each other. The teacher and the colleague's husband pointed and exclaimed in unison: "I know you." We talked together in low voices. We shared each other's dreams. My colleague's husband wept as he concluded his narrative. He looked into the eyes of the teacher.

"I am so sorry that I brought you the telegram. I wish there was something I could have done. I sat at the table all night but had no idea you did what you did upstairs."

The teacher is weeping. I am choked and have put my head in my hands. "So you did that to be with me? Why?" I ask.

"I don't know. Perhaps it was the thought that love would carry over whatever stood between us and that we would be together again."

"Well, I guess *that* has happened. But I don't see any attraction now between us other than the fact that we are here and sharing coincidental dreams that have troubled us for years."

"I don't feel anything either," she replied.

"Perhaps," my colleague's husband said haltingly as tears flowed down his cheeks, "we are here ... leading our own lives ... all we are doing is giving each other permission to forge ahead ... ahead with *this* reality before we go our separate ways ... not to carry grief with us to the end of the world and beyond." Crying, we joined hands and nodded to each other for reassurance.

"Maybe, today, these days, our days here and now, are the good old days we longed for once but never thought we could regain." Everyone nodded, partially in agreement and partially, in a strange way, out of a sense of regret for what we could not bring to resolution, the lives we once had and left behind. We finished our meal, rose, hugged each other, promised to get together again, though that will not likely happen, and went our separate ways.

That night, I arrived home, exhausted and cold, and took the dog for a walk up the Avenue Road hill. As we sat on the couch I rubbed her tummy. "Well, pupsicle, did you have a good day? I missed you." She looked into my eyes and nuzzled closer to my thigh.

I remembered the day I bought her from a farm north of the city. The farmer's wife had two dogs. When she undid the leashes, the other dog ran away but the little black one, who most resembled a border collie, ran up to me and wrapped her front paws around my leg. The dog chose me as if she had always known me. She has followed me around the house and on my travels ever since that day we met, and there are times when I have the strange sense she will always be my dog.

Visitors

I know the decorative oval window half way up the stair-case.

The panes spread out in arms from the centre of the glass in a web pattern.

When sun flowed down the stairs into the parlour, I could have seen a spider shadow cross the rug.

Hollyhocks, blue, yellow, pink, leaned against a trellis in the garden. The parlour was furnished with antique chairs and china vase lamps. Water-colour pictures of wood-land scenes hung on the yellow wall paper. On the mantle there was a clock that ticked and chimed on the hour and the half hour as the shadow of the web crossed the room during a summer afternoon.

A woman who looked like my grandmother was scold-ing me. I had done something wrong. I ran into the bed-room where the hob-tufted spread stretched over the brown antique bed frame. I put my face in the pillow. I did not want to look at her. I never liked to be scolded, espe-cially by someone I did not know.

When the scolding was over I was told I could go outside to the garden. An elderly man was bending over the flower beds. He was picking brown heads from the flowers and tossing them in a galvanized bucket. I bent down to look at the bucket because it reminded me of frost on window panes—the jagged shards gleamed and caught the light.

He said to me: "Stand back or you might get something in your eye." I stood up and followed him to the end of the garden.

There was a shed at the end of the garden scented with turpentine and earth where spider webs stuck to my fingers. The shed was painted dark green inside and out, and on the floor were cans where tears of the paint had run down the side and dried before they reached the ground.

In the corner was a workbench, and a hammer with a round, ball end to it was resting among the other tools —a saw, a rusty chisel. I felt the edge of the wooden workbench.

"Be careful," he said, "you might get a sliver."

We walked back into the house. The woman who was scolding me was drawing a pan of cookies from the oven. The kitchen smelled of gingerbread. The air was sweet. "These will cool by the time your parents get here, and you can take some with you."

I wanted to touch them, but I knew the silver cookie sheet was hot, so I waited.

The yellow kitchen chairs had hoops atop them that were fed with spindles that grew out of the seat. Whoever made the chairs had carved the shape of someone's bottom into the wood.

I ran my hand over the rise and fall of the chair's indentation. "What do you call this?" I asked.

"Chamfering," she replied. "Cham-fer-ing. It makes the hard wood more comfortable."

My mother and father's chairs were upholstered in marbled plastic. They were made of chrome. Outside, in the garden, I heard a crowing. I stood up on the chair seat to look out the window and saw a white hen being chased by a brown and orange rooster. He had a red comb on his head. The hen out-ran him but not before she spread her wings as if trying to fly.

"May I play with the chickens?"

"Get down off the chair before you fall and hurt yourself."

I sat and waited. She placed a glass of milk in front of me on the yellow iron table top. When the cookie was set down, she said: "Only one for now." I gripped the glass of milk in both hands as I had been taught when I was at someone else's house, and drank it slowly.

And when my parents and grandparents came to fetch me home, my grandfather sat with the others in the parlour and cupped his hands in a patch of sunlight on the yellow wallpaper, and the shadow of his fingers took the shape of a spider that climbed the wall among the cabbage roses and settled itself into the web from the window.

Everyone waved goodbye as the car drove away leaving a cloud of dust on the lane behind us. I turned around in the back seat and waved out the rear window, but the man and the woman had already turned away and headed back toward the house. The woman paused for an instant on the porch and wiped her hands on her apron.

When I woke in my own bed that night, I saw a pale beige house-haunter swing from the fixture and drop to the floor. I pulled my feet into the covers.

I've told you about this many times.

I had never been able to be certain whether the place I had been was real or was a dream. Spiders are real. A person is never more than six feet from a spider. I know they are everywhere. They live in both shadows and light. They weave webs.

Are dreams webs?

And if they are webs, what becomes trapped in them? Time? Images? People? Faces?

I often described the dream to members of my family. They would shake their heads. "Yes," they would say, "you must have been dreaming."

But when I told them that our kitchen table was being built in Selkirk, my mother said: "You should drop by Auntie Margaret's old place and take a look. We left you there one weekend when we had to drive to Detroit."

That's why we had to go there on our way to see the cabinet-maker about our table.

He, too, had a house with hollyhocks climbing a post near his door. He, too, had a weathered, dark green shed out back. That's where he did his cabinetry. He invited us in. Just inside the door on a wooden work bench where a set of gleaming chisels were arranged like instruments in an operating theatre, there was a seat he was chamfering. I paused as he made his way to the back of his shed, and ran my hands over the indentations.

He rifled through a stack of wooden boards he had salvaged from old houses in the area that had been torn down or fallen down.

"You can't let the past go to waste."

"No," I said. "They don't make wood like that any more."

He had planed old floor boards. He reached into a galvanized bucket full of water, splashed a handful onto five boards he had laid atop a large work bench. As his hand spread the water, the tiger stripes in the maple caught the light from the cobwebbed four-pane window, and the wood glowed.

"That's your table top. Do you like it?"

I could imagine, couldn't you, sitting there, eating our dinners with our children, perhaps baking ginger bread cookies and mixing the dough on the surface.

"Tiger for the top, birds-eye for the legs," he said. "It will be beautiful."

We sorted through more lumber, and he let us select his finest birds-eye maple from the tangle of webs and boards.

The table is now the centre of our home together. It has done us good service for the past twenty years. We will pass it on to our daughter, and perhaps she will give it to one of her children.

It has been the place we lay our meals and weave our conversations.

After we finished imagining our table into being at the cabinet-maker's farm, we drove along a concession for a few miles and turned right into the mouth of a lane. I had to get out and lift the heavy iron gate from the entrance.

No one had been in the house for many years.

As we approached, I saw the veranda overgrown with vines. There were no hollyhocks to be found. The porch boards were jumbled like the teeth of the old man at the gas station where we had stopped earlier to ask directions.

When he smiled, he nodded, and said: "Yep, I knew them well. All gone now. Long gone."

I tried to look in the glass of the front door, but a lace curtain still hung over the window and barred my view. The front window was also curtained. I wanted to see in. I wanted to look into the past and see if it had been a dream or if it had been real.

I walked around the side of the house and could see into the garden. The green shed had collapsed on itself and I wondered if the ball-peen hammer and the paint cans were still in there, but I did not go to look.

But as I started to come back around the front, I stopped. The oval window was at shoulder height now. I stood on my toes and looked in. A brown and grey wolf spider hung from its web on the outside of the window and stared at me with caution. I did not want to break its web. I put my hand over my eyes to get a better look. The wolf spider climbed the rungs of his trap and waited on the window-frame for me to leave.

I spit on my index finger and cleaned a small portal from the dirt that had accumulated on the glass. The yellow cabbage roses were still in bloom on the walls, although the places where the pictures had been had turned to squares of light, and the mantle clock was not there to count the hours.

"I know this place. I thought I had dreamed it, but it is real. It has changed," I said to you. "Maybe the past is not a dream after all."

Patiently, you wrapped your arms around me. I felt your fingers climb across my neck.

The Cards in Her Hand

My grandparents' house on the maple-lined street is a long way from the bus stop. It is a cold walk on a winter night. I am chilled to the bone when I arrive. As I lean against the radiator in the front hall, my arms and legs begin to warm and I place my boots in the tray with their mouths facing the heat. It is a Thursday night and after dinner with my grandparents I go the final two blocks to the family church for choir practice. It is a long journey for a seven-year-old on his own.

My grandfather, who is deaf, has not heard me arrive as I step into the living room and see him cleaning up the dining room table from the Thursday afternoon bridge club, shuffling the cards back into decks and sweeping crumbs from the family heirloom Irish linen table cloth. I can picture the gathering of grey-haired friends, their jokes spoken loudly so my grandfather can hear. They smile and play their hands—north, south, east, and west —all converging in their elemental concentration as they bid and deal and bid again. I can see the cards in my grandmother's thin hands, her eye brows raised as she examines what she has been dealt.

My grandmother cooks dinner and I play solitaire on the enamelled-top kitchen table before setting our places with the cutlery arranged as I had learned from her. I look up from my cards and tell her she reminds me of the wimpled Queen of Hearts. She dismisses the idea, but I know she is happy that I see her in unexpected places. With my parents, she and my grandfather are the solid cornerstones of my life. North. South. East. West.

Hers has not been an easy life—a Victorian childhood, the First World War, the lists of the war dead on which she found her friends and the boy friends of her chums. She rolled bandages with her friends around the dining room table, and comforted them when they returned to the circle of cloth with their grief still fresh. She had fallen in love with a frail young man from around the corner who cannot hear the shouted commands or distinguish half the colours in the spectrum. He has been turned down for active service, and each week a woman presents him with a white feather when he goes downtown, and each week he goes to the recruiting office and is turned down.

In the early years of their marriage my grandfather saw the old city firms that employed him fall one by one for want of eldest sons to take their helms. Just when they thought the hardship might have passed, there was the Great Depression, that draughty hallway of a decade when there was never enough coal in the cellar to keep the boiler hot. And just when she and my grandfather thought they were clear of the trials and tribulations of the world, another war came and took the sons of their friends. My grandfather sits every evening with the remaining hearing of his good ear tuned to the blaring vacuum-tubed radio. And when his nose tells him that dinner is ready, he pulls himself up from his armchair and joins us at the table. The smell of baking always fills the house.

Food—the recipes, the tastes, the old cravings—is the one thing that remains faithful to a person throughout life. As long as the familiar dishes are there, a person feels rooted in their blessing. The food at my grandparents' kitchen table is simple and honest. It is a food that comes from the heart and sticks to the ribs to give comfort on a cold night. Meatloaf topped with bacon strips, mashed potatoes with thick tomato gravy, creamed celery, and to top it off snow pudding and sugar cookies, and strong black tea with a little milk to soften its edge.

Perhaps because I am hungry now, I go rummaging for the small red box that sat on my grandmother's kitchen counter on those nights when I would arrive cold and hungry. My mother gave it to me to take to grad school. She imagined I would be cooking for myself, but I never got around to opening it or putting its secrets to work. When I was hungry I would boil a hot dog or go for some fast food. I know that in the red box are the secrets that made my grandmother's dinners so special, menus and recipes conjured from the heart of simplicity because their magic was called forth by love and patience and the warmth of a well-used kitchen on a winter night.

I shut my eyes, just as my grandmother used to draw down the dark green black-out blinds after the dishes were done and the kitchen was settled for the night. I am a ghost that has arrived in the past. I stand beside my grandmother as she is patting a meatloaf into shape. My grandfather is listening to the late afternoon radio shows, and

I have not yet arrived at their house. She holds the high-sided silver pan in her hands as if it is a jewel box and sets it on top of the stove to open the oven and slide it in. Making food was her ritual, and I want to stand and watch how the rest of the meal is made and try to recognize what it means when someone says they put love into their cooking, but I am brought back to reality.

My wife calls down the stairs and asks me what I am looking for. I tell her I am looking for the secret ingredients of my past. Together we shuffle the plastic bins from side to side in the store room until we find the one that contains the red box.

"I am going to write a short story that presents my grandmother's recipes. I want to show my writing class that stories can be useful."

"May I suggest that before you do that, you try them?" My wife is wise in these things. "You don't want the story to poison anyone."

We take the box up to our kitchen and open it as if it is a reliquary. I sort through the neat filing cards. Some recipes are scraps torn from newspapers or magazines. "Here is the one for sugar cookies," I say, holding it up as if a rare pearl.

The card is written in an elegant secretarial cursive. The flourish of the capital letters harkens back to a time when people cared not only about what they said but how they presented themselves to others through the written word. In an age of cares, they took care in what they did. My grandmother's handwriting, those cards in her hand and the details of the ingredients in each recipe, tells me that her cooking *was* an act of love. As I hold the cards in my hands, I am standing beside her watching as each item is sifted carefully and mixed in her favourite bowl on her enamel table top, each ingredient a small note in an opus she composes.

"I am going to begin with the end of the meal," I tell my wife as I lay the butter, flour, and sugar on the table. Dessert must always be made first because the conclusion of a solid meal takes the longest to make, and it must be as memorable as a farewell kiss.

Sugar Cookies

1 cup shortening (butter)
1 cup granulated sugar
2 eggs
2 ½ cups all purpose flour
1 tsp baking soda
1 ½ tsp cream of tartar
½ tsp salt
1 tsp lemon extract or almond extract

Method:

Cream shortening and cream in the sugar gradually. Beat in the eggs. Mix and sift together the dry ingredients and add to the creamed mixture together with the lemon or almond extract. Mix well. Drop by teaspoons on an ungreased baking sheet. Flatten with the bottom of a glass dipped in sugar. Sprinkle with white sugar. Bake in a moderate oven 375 Fahrenheit about ten minutes.

Makes five dozen.

The cookies turn out well enough though there is something missing in them that I seem to remember. I have been impatient in my work because I desire to bring the lost taste back to life, and I have rushed the patient process of mixing and stirring. "Love suffereth long and is kind," my grandmother would say as she blended the mixture with her wooden spoon and turned the bowl to scrape the clingings from the side.

I once decided to hide inside my grandmother's kitchen cupboard with the cookie tin all to myself. The tin was adorned with pictures of English crowns. It was a memento of Elizabeth II's coronation and an emblem of my grandmother's attachment to "the old country," though she had been born and raised in Canada and never set foot overseas. I had pulled the cupboard door shut behind me. She came into the kitchen to find a baking pan she was about to loan to a friend, and when she bent down and opened the door I said 'hello' to cover my guilt. The shock sent her to her knees, gasping. I was cut off from the wonderful cookies for a week, and that seemed an awfully long time. If I was good, I would be given a third cookie at the end of dinner, and if I was especially good I was allowed to take a fourth one home with me. The cookie never lasted past the first block on the drive home.

As the last tray of the five dozen comes out of the oven and the air is sweet with a tart vanilla bouquet, snow is falling on our backyard. Light from our kitchen window spreads across the garden and the gentle rolls of drifts in the illuminated beds and plantings reminds me of snow pudding.

Snow Pudding was the dessert she loved to serve me.

This old Canadian dish is a delicious misnomer. It is neither snow nor a pudding as one might expect. It is a lemon
and gelatin concoction covered in a creamy custard sauce.
My grandmother always loved to tell me of Victorian picnics beside the Don River when the favourite finale to an
outdoor meal was lemon snow with custard. The ingredients would be packed in crushed ice, and when the ice
was just going soft was the moment the dessert would be
served beneath the branches of weeping willows. On the
tongue it is cool and refreshing, but just as the taste of
lemon tang appears to speak, it vanishes as if a memory
I cannot quite bring to life. It is a dessert of ghosts.

During my childhood, I loved the pudding but was
not wild about the custard. My sister did not like the pudding but loved the custard. It was a good arrangement.
Whenever we were sick, my grandmother would send up
bowls of snow and Mason jars of yellow custard to put us
back on our feet. I scan the recipe card and notice that the
pudding and the custard share a sense of economy; one
requires yolks, the other the whites. During the Second
World War when everyone was issued ration books, a
clever cook could make several dishes with very limited
ingredients. Meat, eggs, bread, and dairy were 'kept back'
to feed the troops. What one was permitted to buy had to
go a long way. Snow pudding and custard sauce were as
much about making the most out of the least as they were
about the taste and sweetness on the tongue. The snow
required just as much sugar as might be left over from a
week's allotment after coffee and other baking had taken
their share. I knew by the pride and patience my grandmother took in making sugar cookies that she had not

been able to make them during those six long years when the black out blinds were drawn down at four o'clock. When she was able to bake it was because she was able to trade something else with a diabetic woman who lived down the street. But even in times of shortage, snow pudding had been possible.

Snow Pudding and Custard Sauce

1 quantity of lemon jelly recipe
1 egg white
⅛ tsp salt

Lemon jelly:

1 ½ tbsp of gelatin
⅓ cup cold water
½ cup granulated sugar
1 ⅓ cups hot water
⅓ cup lemon juice
Thin shavings of lemon rind

Method for lemon jelly:

Soak the gelatin in cold water. Combine sugar, hot water, and lemon rind, boil together for two minutes. Strain out the rind. Pour this over the gelatin and stir until the gelatin is dissolved. Then add the strained lemon juice.

Method for Lemon snow:

After the lemon jelly has set, when partially set, beat the lemon jelly until foamy. Add salt to the egg white and beat until stiff. Add this to the beaten jelly beating it in well. Allow the mixture to set. Lift out in spoonfuls into sherbet glasses. Serve with custard sauce.

Serves Six.

Custard Sauce:

1 ¼ scalded milk (heated to hot without boiling)
2 ½ tbsp sugar
1 tsp corn starch
⅛ tsp salt
2 egg yolks slightly beaten
¼ cup cold milk
¼ tsp vanilla

Method:

Scald the milk. Combine sugar, corn starch, salt, and egg yolks with the cold milk. Add this to the scalded milk. Cook stirring constantly until thick. Add the vanilla. Chill. Before chilling add a piece of wax paper to the top to avoid a skin.

The scalding of milk sounds painful. Scalding was a more common occurrence in kitchens than it is today. Now, if we want something, we microwave it and know enough to let the seconds run down before removing the cover.

My grandmother had her arm in a bandage one evening when I arrived because the celery water had splashed her while she was draining the pot. She made no fuss about it, but I could tell by the way her other hand tried to cover it as we talked over dessert that she was in pain. That is what scalding means in one sense. In the other sense, it is merely about bringing the milk to the verge of boiling and then pulling it off so it will not talk itself into a heavy taste and a thick skin.

After some thought as I muddle around my kitchen, I decide to substitute the made-from-scratch lemon gelatin with Jell-O. I feel as if I am cheating, in a small way betraying, the sanctity of what is written on the cards, though before I turn in for the night and let the jelly set I shave in some lemon rind and squeeze a little juice into the liquid. I know that during the night the elements will mix and the taste of lemon will prevail over all the other ingredients. In the morning, a day when I am not teaching, the snow is a brilliant white with blue shadows in the yard, and I mix the jelly with the egg whites until they are almost identical to the layer of new fallen snow that drapes from the branches of our pine trees. Before I let it set again, I scoop up a mouthful and stare at the spoon before putting it in my mouth. It is almost snow pudding, but it is missing something, and again, I don't know what it is.

One evening my grandfather raised his spoon as he lapped up the snow and told me how he had spent his winter days as a boy. He lived on the lip of the Don Valley. In the winter, there was always a rink on the flats below his home. He and his chums would come home from school, deliver their papers quickly while there was still daylight, and then toboggan down the steep hill with their skates slung over their shoulders. Their mothers, being good and thoughtful souls, would stuff baked potatoes into the toes of the skates. When they donned their skates, their shoes were kept warm by the spuds. On their climb back up the hill, they would take the edge off their appetites—they always worked up good ones in the open air of the rink —and eat the potatoes and toss the skins over their shoulders. As the snow melted and the grass emerged in the late months of winter, the hillside would be littered with the last evidence of the potato shells as they bled back into the earth from which they had come. Spring would emerge green and tender. The colour green makes me think about creamed celery.

What I love about creamed celery is not merely its texture in the mouth, but what it means to prepare it. I strip the stalks from the bundle and pare the back of each miniature tree of life to remove the strings and tethers that would toughen it and make it worldly. Paring celery always suggests a freeing of the stalks from their own bounds. And as I work my way through the bunch, I realize that I am nearer and nearer to the heart. At the core of a bunch of celery are delicate stems and childlike yellow leaves that are small replicas of the whole celery. The main stalks stand around it, protecting the heart from the chill of the refrigerator, from the bumps and bruises of the world the way families look after their children.

After cutting the larger stems into bite-sized pieces, I begin the cream sauce. It is called a *roux* or more commonly a *rue*. That word haunts me. I want to rue the word itself. A *rue* in cooking is merely butter and flour, a means to an end, a cornerstone upon which a soup or a sauce is built. It speaks of the pain a person must endure sometimes in order to achieve something finer, the way great things often start with simple foundations. As words go, *rue* is one of the most ambiguous and ambivalent words. In French it means a street, an avenue, a conduit that will lead somewhere in the same way that every day leads to a different place in time and life. It also means 'regret' in English, the haunting presence of the sin of omission, of what was not said to someone as they lay dying, what was not within the comfort zone of a person in an important instant before the moment was lost. I arrived too late at my grandmother's deathbed to say goodbye. I rue the day I was delayed.

My grandmother told me a story of Teddy Roosevelt's visit to town during the First World War. He made his speech in the red stone castle of the old Armoury just weeks before he passed into history. He had argued that the United States needed to be in the war. "We shall *rue* the day we left our fellow English-speakers in peril." That was what rue meant to me as a child. Teddy Roosevelt. The obligation to history shared among friends. There it is in the card in her hand. The spelling is hers. She loved to cook and never learned a word of French. Not *roux*, but *rue*. Her culinary skills were acquired by watching her mother, and her mother's skills were learned in Ireland from her mother and grandmother. The simple paste at the base of a cream sauce was an ancient art passed from generation to generation. I wish I had paid more attention to my grandmother when she was cooking.

To make a roux one must follow the 2-2-1 principle.

Two cups of flour, two cups of milk, and one teaspoon of butter. After the celery has boiled to a delicate softness, I set the pot aside. I need to use at least a portion of a cup as a vegetable stock to add to the milk to cut the heaviness of the sauce. I slowly stir the flour into the melting butter in the pot, letting the ingredients thicken as if by magic. Then, I gradually add the celery water and milk to the roux and stir it slowly over low heat until it thickens. I toss in a little salt, a little pepper to ripen the taste, and the drained celery. As I look out the kitchen window, I am again reminded that the food one eats is often a reflection of where one lives. Some would call that a confusion of the senses, a form of synaesthesia. I call it the poetry of life. The white and the soft green are there in the boughs of the trees beside the patio where the chickadees are darting in and out of the barren hydrangea tree. They are hungry but very much alive on a cold day, and I will fill their feeder when I am finished my cooking.

The meatloaf is next on my agenda. Out of the corner of my eye I see my microwave oven beckoning to me but I know that it is out of bounds if I am to be true to the past. In the cupboard under the countertop, a place where I might have hidden with a cookie tin when I was small, I root around and discover that I still have my grandmother's meatloaf pan. The sides are undented and square. The meat is cold around my fingers. I knead the bread crumbs with the chopped celery and tomato chili sauce, which is not my grandmother's famous fruit chili sauce that she laid in bottles in her cellar every harvest but a bottle of local preserve I picked up at an organic farmer's market. A pain shoots through my hands and reaches into my brain.

My grandmother had arthritis. She also had an upright piano in her living room, and as she grew older the piano grew more silent. Life perpetually takes away those things that one loves, and though the music stopped as she grew older, the meatloaves did not. She was willing to bear the pain to make this dish. If anything, the meatloaves became more resonant in their taste, more determined to fill an empty stomach on a winter night, and more beautiful in their aroma as time passed. My choir days and the Thursday night meals with my grandparents came to an end when my grandfather passed away. After he left us I felt I should not impose on my grandmother. I was older. I could come and go on the bus with confidence, and instead of joining my grandmother at the table, I left another empty place for my grandmother to face and ate unmemorable burgers with my friends at a local greasy spoon. I also gave up singing. On my last evening in the choir, I stood alone after the other choristers had left, and sang a few bars to the empty church and listened as my voice echoed into silence. I thought of my grandfather who never heard a note I sang because of his deafness. By the next autumn, my voice had changed. When my grandmother passed away, I didn't have anyone to sing for anymore.

To love someone is to suffer pain for them, not just to experience joy. I held my daughter aloft to watch the Santa Claus Parade and the ache in my shoulder made me think of my grandmother's arthritic hands kneading the cold ground meat for the weekly meatloaf I loved. The card with my grandmother's recipe for her weekly meatloaf has my name written on top of it with a little star beside it and the word 'favourite.' As was the case with the other recipes, I made the meatloaf to recreate the choir night meals, but there was something missing in everything. I often asked her what her secret ingredient was—I had heard a commercial on television where someone kidded about having an ancient secret to a dish. Her answer was always the same. "I put love in it for you." But what does love taste like? Is it less or more salt? Is it the flavour of a person's hands as they feed the ingredients into a mixing bowl? Is it the patience a person takes with what they do, or the familiarity they possess with a recipe? She knew what I loved and wanted to give me that love in the patience, honesty, and the even the pain of what she made. I could taste it.

Meatloaf

1 lb lean ground beef
1 ½ of cornflake crumbs
1 egg beaten
1 cup chopped celery
¼ cup chopped onion or shallots
Some chopped red pepper
Bacon strips
¼ cup chili sauce
Salt and pepper to taste.

Method:

Grease pan. Top mixture with bacon strips. Bake in 350 over for 45 to 50 mins. Look at it every now and then.

Serves 4.

I look at the card and I am puzzled as to who the fourth person is. I know for certain that nothing went to waste at my grandparent's house. Perhaps they split the extra piece with each other over lunch the next day, a poached egg, and a piece of toast on the plate to keep the meatloaf company. As I grew older and could eat more, I was always offered seconds and never turned them down. There was a hunger inside me that I could not satisfy. That same hunger was what drove me to find the recipe. I wanted to know if the tastes could still sustain me and whether they were worth sharing with others, not merely as a recollection but as an instruction in how to describe and write about what a person finds meaningful in life.

During the week of my rummaging for the recipe cards, my wife and daughter test the creamed celery, the meatloaf, the snow pudding. My daughter loves lemon things and begs me to make the snow again. My wife loves the custard. I see the smiles on their faces as they ask for more. The sugar cookies disappear one afternoon when my daughter's friends come over to play video games and to text message each other even though they are in the same room.

Though the world of infinite possibilities collapses around me as I grow older, I still hold the cards in my grandmother's hand, the cards that she was dealt, and that she played not merely to win a game but to make the playing of the game beautiful. I understand just how she played them to make the most of what she was given. I try to tell my daughter about the dishes and about the nature of frugality she will eventually have to learn, if not during her student days on a tight budget then in her life after college when survival is not merely an obligation to others but an art one learns. Learning to use everything life gives one is a language in which the word love is said over and over again to fill the mouths of others.

I take my kitchen handiwork into my class. My students are a tough audience who want to create something but have no idea how to go about it and often resent those who try to show them. I begin by telling the class that fiction is not merely making up stuff but about making something.

"Let's say a story told you something you could use, something that could be useful to you to help you through a day. Let's examine the idea that a story could feed you and warm you up inside or make you realize how much you loved someone or how they loved you."

I lay out the spread on a paper table cloth and set plastic cutlery and paper plates before them. "I am going to read you a story you can eat as an example of what we are discussing today. It is called 'The Cards in Her Hand.' For your assignment this week, I want you to write your own story not about food that has been passed to you out of a drive-thru window but about food you want to share with others because it is out of the ordinary, food that feeds your thoughts and your imaginations, that offers you something other than just junk inside you, food you connect with love and the people who have loved you and the magic you would want to pass on to others." Some of the students in the back row roll their eyes.

"Stories are as much about real things that you know and experience as they are about what you make up. You don't have to recycle the plots of video games or same-old-same-old television shows. Look into your own lives and make a story, piece by piece, ingredient by ingredient. Balance it, so it offers a variety of tastes and surprises and recalls things you might have forgotten or that others have long overlooked. You have mouths and minds to feed with ideas, right? Those ideas come from you. They can be made and remade over and over again, always new, always fresh if you can find the recipe."

A boy in a reversed baseball cap shakes his head as if I have lost my mind.

"Man, I only eat hot dogs and Kraft Dinner," he says.

But I refuse to let his food choices be the point I am trying to make. He needs to be fed but he is starved inside, maybe not physically but in the realm of discovery. He is speaking through the hunger of his mind that has not yet learned how to feed itself. To live is to fuel the imagination as well as the body, and at the same time to feed the body is to enable the imagination. "Your choice. You can taste it or you can just guess what it tastes like. That said, guessing at something is not what makes for good fiction. Come and get it. You don't have to try it, but here it is if you want it."

A braver student shuffles up to the front of the classroom and picks up a paper plate and cutlery. I continue with the challenge of the assignment. "Read the tastes, the textures, the simplicity that is spoken through what you take into yourselves." I try to persuade them. "All the experience in life is waiting to speak to you if you will let it. Your obligation as writers is to enable others to enter into what you have known, and to know what you have loved, lost and tried to regain." A few more come to the front and gather around the spread.

A young woman with a round face and rosy cheeks takes a bite from the snow pudding and it melts in her mouth. Her face glows with wonder and surprise as she tries to speak to me. She swallows and exclaims: "I had a word for it for a moment, and then it was gone. It was … it was …oh, what's the word…like turning over a lucky card in a game of chance or finding someone in a crowd I had thought was gone from my life. It was…it was like the first warm day of spring when everything comes back to life. You know what I mean?" I nod.

There must be a word for it, but I can't find it. I shall go home and search through the cards to see if my grandmother wrote it down on the back of something she loved to make.

Catchers

Paul described all this to Luke though he was certain his lover could not hear him. One of the stories was about hair, long hair, and how an old man in a tower would let the blond lengths of it down to street level to entice beautiful young men to climb up to his apartment. When the young men reached the top, the hair was white as blank paper. Paul had seen pictures of eccentrics in India who never cut their hair during their entire lifetimes. The ends were the colour a person's hair had been in youth. The grey would appear partway up the strands, and then fade into the white of old age where they reached the man who, by then, would be old bones. By the time the climbers were at the top, Paul said, it was too late to turn back.

Luke was dying and had given up shaving. He had started a beard before the invader came to live inside him, but now that he was in his final days, weakened by the presence that trashed his life from within, Paul wanted to reclaim the Luke he had loved when they were both young men. Paul wanted to find the man who lay beneath the matted tangle.

With scissors, at first, then carefully with a straight-edge so as not to draw any blood into the white lather through which the bristles sprang, Paul began to shave his partner's face. The razor scraped the growth down to the flesh—cheeks, hands, and the pale chest hidden beneath the dirty red t-shirt Luke refused to launder. In the days before the silence overtook him, Luke told Paul the shirt was lucky and argued the only way it would come off was if the undertaker cut it off with a pair of scissors. Like the hair, it was an extra layer of armour Luke had donned in his fight against death.

Years before, when the hair and moustache were shorter, Luke reminded Paul of Einstein—hairier, though with the same sympathy in the eyes that were so beautiful. Now that Luke was gaunt and skeletal, the eyes were the one thing that continued to speak of the man that once was. Gentle and deep, the eyes protruded now and did not look at Paul as much as they looked into and through him. And though that look frightened Paul, he saw what the young men had seen when Luke caught them in the moonlight.

Luke and Paul had been together for forty years. And as it had been in the beginning, Paul continued to tell Luke stories to amuse him, to keep the blood running through Luke's veins, though gradually, as each day passed, life wanted less and less a part of Luke. The stories were mostly nightmares. Luke loved the terrors that tumbled through his brain. If he woke, sweating and exhausted from having been part of them, they were good stories. The earliest stories had been about beautiful young knights who went into the enchanted forest and fell in love, not with the vacuous princesses of court, but with each other, and on returning to the world of the disenchanted, slew the dragons that breathed fire on those who loved each other. Such stories were beautiful to them, and drew them closer, and made them weep.

They had marched together on their crusade during the early days of the cause before the city that now embraced them and forgot them in its embrace was unwilling to accept who they were. They fought the blue-uniformed catchers at the bath houses. They ran from the night sticks and the paddy-wagons and hid in the darkness. The more they lived, the more the two men knew the scars of the fight. Those early days had been the days of the Knights' tales. But now, with the politicians turning out in glitter to glad-hand sweaty palms on a brilliant summer afternoon when everyone celebrated everything except the truth that Luke and Paul had come to know, the stories were harder to tell and became more terrifying. Paul's stories scared their friends, but Luke always wanted to hear more. Sometimes Paul would play the piano to add music to the tales. Luke told Paul that those the stories were the record of their lives together, the promise that as long as the narratives continued their relationship would live. That is why Paul told them, and kept telling them, even when they were certain that one was speaking and the other was beyond hearing. Paul found it hard to tell his stories when the snow of their last winter together fell with the silence that snow brings.

The previous winter had been the hardest. Luke was mobile then. The invader had not yet settled in his spine, and when the moon shone through the glass of their balcony doors in the dawn hours of still February mornings, Luke would wake and pine to be let out to visit his shadows. Paul would delay him as long as he could with stories that made Luke smile; but inevitably, Luke would go out.

Paul would follow him at a safe distance through the ice-covered alleyways behind Church Street. The longer Paul could keep Luke at home, the less likely it was that his partner would find a stray staggering in the darkness, a helpless straggler who either had no home or could not return to one he knew. Paul would follow at a safe distance. Luke would approach the stray young man, and Paul would remain in the shadows though he could often see the streetlight or the light from a window reflected in the eyes of the straggler. When Luke would return home at dawn, he would ask Paul to tell him the story of how the man dog came into being. Paul knew that, if Luke woke, he would want to hear that story again.

Luke did wake from his sleep. He had not woken for five days. Paul thought Luke's last words were going to be about wanting to smell steak cooking in the kitchen. Paul grilled another so the aroma would please Luke, but when he returned to ask Luke what he thought of the steak he found his partner unresponsive. That had been more than two weeks ago. Paul could not remember exactly, though. Luke's breathing was a series of gasps. They were awful. They sounded hollow. Paul had promised Luke a death at home and no matter how his loved one suffered, he had to remain true to that promise.

Couples gathered in the bars and restaurants along the main drag for their Friday night revels. Paul could hear the traffic and voices from the street below. Music came from one of the bars. The dark hours of the morning before the sunrise, after the restaurants had shuttered and the bars had turned off their lights, would have been Luke's time to go out. As Paul entered the room to sit by his partner and listen to the sound of his laboured breathing fade into the night, Luke spoke. He asked if the steak had been good. The question startled Paul. The nearly dead are not supposed to speak when they are given up for dead. Perhaps this is what is known as the final rally. He asked Paul to tell him a story. Paul pulled drew a chair closer to Luke's bed so he could bend over and whisper the story.

Once upon a time, Paul began, there was a little boy who loved to dress in red capes like the one he had found in a baker's shop where they made buttery crescent rolls and warm buns each morning before dawn. The boy would go out in the darkness to prowl, for the hour or so before dawn is when one sees the shadows of the dead and dances with them. It is the hour when bakers rise to bake, when the first delivery trucks of vegetables arrive at the shuttered restaurants, when the emptiness of the streets makes one think that the world has died, and when the last lights from windows reveal lovers standing pressed against each other. Four in the morning was when the boy smelled the crescent rolls in the oven. They sprang to life magically in his senses as the first sign of day even before the sun rose.

The baker had left one of his shop windows partially opened to cool off the room where he floured the table and stirred the mixing bowls to feed the enormous oven. The boy slipped into the shop, enticed by the scent that curled into the street. Though the rolls seemed to be magic to his nose and his stomach, they were not what he took from the baker.

Instead of stealing the rolls on the cooling rack, as he thought he would, the boy's eye caught a bundle of red clothes the baker had left just inside the shop door. Rolls, no matter how magic they might seem, would only last a day. Clothes could last a long time. The red clothes were made of satin, and the boy ran his fingers over them to feel how smooth they were as they caught the light of the dying moon trying to hide before the sun came looking for it with a vengeance to catch it and kill it. The boy crawled out through the partially opened window and took the clothes to a packing crate he called home behind the piano store.

When the boy woke, he was hungry and wished he had stolen the rolls. He had fallen asleep but only briefly. His hunger had woken him. But his neck did not hurt because his head had been pillowed by the red bundle, and while he slept he had the most amazing dreams about flying, about becoming invisible, and of growing fangs and running through the woods as the starlight filled his head. He opened the bundle. A pair of trousers and a tight crimson top tumbled onto the floor of the piano crate, but best of all there was a hooded cowl and a mask that covered all but the eyes and gave him the appearance of a wolf. The boy put on the outfit. It would have been too small for the baker. It fit the boy perfectly. It became his second skin.

The next night, when the bars and restaurants were closing, and the moon was rising over the streets as he ran toward the valley at the city's edge—he always sensed he ran faster at night than during the day—the moon followed him until he reached the woods in the hollow. He saw the outline of the baker in the distance, shuffling along the path others had worn between the trees. But he had heard the baker had died the day before, had dropped dead in a frenzy while looking for his red costume and its wolf-like cowl that he wore when he went into the woods. When the boy saw the baker's ghost, he thought the man had fallen into a box of flour. The baker was chuffing toward a ramshackle house in the clearing ahead. The boy thought it odd that the baker would be heading away from town at the hour when he would be going in the opposite direction to begin his day's work, but the dead go to the woods and ponder their lives by moonlight and reflect on their shadows among the trees and fungal stumps.

The baker was carrying a basket overflowing with rolls, so crammed that one crescent toppled out onto the path, and the baker stopped and kicked it under a clump of ferns. It had been meant as food for the dead—the baker's dead lover who waited for him in the woods for years. But the boy was eager to follow the baker, not for loose rolls but for the aroma. The scent was even more intense among the trees than it had been in the bakery. It filled the boy's senses and turned his brain into fire. A moment later, the boy found himself on top of the baker. The baker, at first, had not resisted because he was already a ghost, but he became annoyed and tried to tell the boy that the rolls were his, but no sound came out. The baker's ghost sat down on a stump and cried while the boy ran off with the last baked goods his baker's hands had made.

Having strewn the rolls in a trail of crumbs so he could find his way out of the forest if the clouds covered the moon, the boy arrived at the small cottage that was the baker's destination. The dwelling was one of the old mail order houses from the Twenties, but it had fallen into disrepair. The paint was peeling off the veranda, the railings and shingles that had once been yellow were brown and rotting in the blue shadows.

The door was unlocked so the boy let himself in. He recognized the old man's voice that called from a room at the back because it had the same dead rasp as the baker's. The voice was asking if the baker had brought him his favourite buns. The boy stood in the doorway of the old man's room, still clutching the baker's basket. The old man smiled. That was the last the boy remembered or wanted to remember, though later, when dawn had come and he had returned to his piano crate in the alley, he remembered how the old man's skin was soft yet creped, its draped flesh sagging from the dead bones. He recalled the aroma that disappeared from the rolls as they cooled. The rolls had left a trail of bread crumbs all the way home. They had stuck to his cape and fallen off as he ran from the old man's house. He tried to follow them, but he heard the catchers coming close, and he hid breathlessly in the underbrush, not knowing which way was out of the labyrinth of trees.

When the sun came up, he took a guess and followed a trail of current buns that someone had made before him—possibly the piano man who knew the forest better than he did—and with a stroke of luck, found his way back to town. Forests are full of bread crumb trails and most are like the invader that gets inside a person. Very few are worth following and even fewer lead to anything more than death.

Luke muttered that he did not want to know what would come next. He did not want to hear about the catcher who would find the boy and take him to a brightly lit room where the catcher would question and question him until he broke down and sobbed a false confession about stealing rolls and murdering bakers and old men. Through mumbles, he asked Paul to tell him another one, a different one, though Paul had to lean into him to hear because his partner's voice was weak and raspy from disuse and from the invader inside him. Luke whispered that he knew there were always two shadows following the boy in the red cape: the catcher, and the piano man who once owned the crate. One would do him harm, and the other would lead him back to his hideaway behind the piano store.

Paul asked if he wanted to hear the story about the first Prince of Wales, and how the king, on discovering his son's cradle overturned and the English collie standing by it, slew the dog, though the dog had saved the baby from a snake and dragged the child to safety. Paul added that the child never smiled again. Luke replied that the story was no fair to the dog, and then he closed his eyes, and returned to sleep. Paul had wanted to tell him that the story would be different this time, that the dog would kill the king and initiate a line of dog despots who would rule over England until their blood-lineage was watered down to short-legged Corgis that simply yapped for applause. Luke would have liked that, but he was unconscious, and his breathing grew laboured and hollow.

Luke's sleep was long and deep after the story of the boy in the red cape. Paul could not remember how many days Luke had been asleep. Paul began to wonder where Luke's dreams were taking him. Maybe Luke was retracing his steps through the back alleys behind the main drag, with Paul not far behind, until the morning nurse came to change the IV.

After several hours when Luke said nothing, and his gasps became chortles, Paul took a needle from his sewing basket and pricked Luke's thumb to see if he was still feeling anything, but Luke woke, and in a far away voice distant from life whispered to Paul that he was not Sleeping Beauty. He then asked why the stories had stopped.

There were many summer nights, Paul recalled. The air was heavy with humidity before a downpour washed the night away into the shining gutters. The leaves updrafted on maples. They rattled like bones or the whispers of those who saw and knew what Luke had done in Paul's stories, the faces that populated Luke's imagination but dared not speak of it to each other. The fair-minded wanted justice, but the thrill of knowing that someone was running, someone was in the streets living not out of the dream but beyond it, and beyond any law or stricture, was almost mouth-watering. The dream was real to them, as real as it was to Luke and Paul. So, Paul continued his story ...

The moon would appear from behind a cloud, and Paul's long-haired lover would scratch at the door to get out. Paul knew Luke had once owned a red Irish setter, an excitable dog that would scratch at the door, wanting out for a run in the middle of the night. Luke had loved that dog until one of the neighbours from the old days shot it with a cross bow.

Luke had never wanted revenge against the neighbour. His friends of the time told him to nail the neighbour's doors shut and set the house on fire, but Luke had simply ignored that temptation. Vengeance would prove nothing. Instead, he tried to remember what the dog had seen and done as he wandered out alone at night. The good boy must have been aware that he was being watched by the catcher, but there was always someone who would bend and pet the dog, not prey but a friend, and sometimes the friend would have a piece of freeze-dried steak in his pocket to feed the setter. But when the dog hungered, the red dog, the boy in the red cape, both good boys wanting to be petted and loved—he would bare his fangs at the smaller, helpless dogs, the ones that men carried in their purses or tucked under their arms at cash registers. They were white, fearful, and uncertain. They yapped and barked, but said nothing. Those were the dogs the setter wanted to claim. They were dogs that had no business being out at night.

Paul had followed Luke on his runs in the night not merely because he acted as lookout when Luke overtook the boys who at first welcomed the advances but then became terrified. Paul would watch as Luke would turn and glance over his shoulder to make sure the catcher was not nearby.

But the catcher was always out there. If it could not collar a fast, good boy, it would find a way to take him down from inside.

That was the way Luke explained it.

They were cruel beings, those catchers. They wore navy blue uniforms to hide themselves in the darkness. They passed from one person to another in the darkness. They would go straight for the blood. They carried rule books in their back pockets, lists of things to do and not do, scrolls of medications and tests they could recite chapter and verse.

If Luke got ahead and disappeared from sight, Paul would go directly home, wait anxiously, meet his exhausted friend at the apartment door. Paul would stick his head out the apartment door and look up and down the silent hallway to make sure Luke had not been followed by a catcher. Often, Luke would come home soaked, having cleaned himself with someone's garden hose or in a backyard fountain.

When they were both certain that the invader was with them for the long-haul, Luke would sit down each morning to his breakfast of champions—a dish of a dozen or more pills of various colours—with a new story from Paul told over eggs Benedict.

Paul would conjure the characters who went into the forest, but unlike those in the old fairy tales, they would never emerge because the forest belongs to the dead. There was always something larger in the brambles, something far more emphatic than a wolf or a bear, something to hate as much as porridge. Paul knew Luke hated porridge. The story would always end with the boy in the red cape returning home to the piano man who would rub his hair as the boy laid his head on the piano man's knee. The piano man would stare down at the boy, tell him he was a good boy, and remind him to go to sleep after a long night. The piano man would play Brahms' *Waltz in A Flat* as the boy in the red cape would fall asleep. The piano man would assure the boy in the red cape that the catcher would not catch him though many nights he came close, that the boy in the cape was invincible and imperishable, and that no matter who or what came to visit him and tear his world apart from inside, the piano man would always be there to rescue him from harm.

The story came to an end. Paul had been holding Luke's hand all night until a breathless silence fell upon the room. It was four a.m. when Paul stood up, walked into the living room of their apartment, sat down at the baby grand that almost filled the window, and softly played the notes of their favourite waltz. Paul closed his eyes and saw a vision that would make the start of a good story, an image of sinking moonlight that once upon a time had broken through the grey clouds.

Chance

Once Upon a Time ...

There was a castle that stood on the shores of a beautiful, shimmering lake where young men and young women went to experience the possibilities of enchantment and happily-ever-afters. To those who had been there and danced the night away, the castle was nothing more than the old, turreted home of a Victorian lumber baron who transformed the stately first growth forests of the Haliburton highlands into hills of saplings and knuckles of moss-patched rolling outcrops. Only the lakes remained. When his grandsons inherited the estate and the hard-scrabble landscape around it, they took their chances and built a pier far out into the lake and set a dancehall there as the crown jewel of their resort.

There was also a time when the world of Toronto society was a small place, so small that chance took up where acquaintance left off in bringing people together. But most of the time, it was acquaintance that brought couples together so that life in the city became a matter of life among people who were and always would be familiars.

For those who found social familiarity troubling—some say it can lead to contempt—the alternative for meeting eligible others was chance, and there was still enough room in the social web of Muddy York for a footprint on a garden path to become a glass slipper. Even if families had known each other for generations, sailed to this land aboard the same ships, built and walked the same streets for almost a century, the world of Toronto society was still small enough in some ways for people to almost meet but not until they permitted chance to intervene and guide their destiny. In order to let chance take its course, there had to be special places where, in the magic of a late summer night and a full moon shimmering on a northern lake, the stiff and proper world of the city would let down its guard and let nature take its course.

In A Land Far, Far Away ...
The Wendigo Inn was advertised as a place for young people to get-away for a magical week off from the offices and corridors and the crowded buses that crisscrossed the grid of the city. It was not far from Toronto, yet just far enough as to seem away, and that is what attracted the young secretary as she sat at her desk in the Conservatory of Music one spring evening and decided that her week-long vacation in September would be spent on the shores of the glistening lake. The Inn was known for its beautiful trails where, if a young couple were to meet, they could get to know each other during casual strolls. There were rocks that nature had placed very carefully where they could sit and talk in the bright summer sun without having to be completely out of sight and completely out

of the range of propriety as their relationship blossomed. It was paradise, just an hour or so's drive from the commotion of daily life.

During the day, large mahogany launches—artefacts of the Twenties and Thirties when the north was opening and lodges were booming—would take the young people out fishing together or for group picnics to a private island on the lake. There were hiking expeditions, horses for riding, and talks on various subjects of interest that were delivered by experts from Toronto. But the highlight of each day was the dance in the hall on the pier, and the highlight of the highlight was the Paul Jones.

The Paul Jones dance was a magical wheel of fortune. It was the roulette wheel of introductions. The women would join hands and form a circle that revolved clockwise when the music started. The men, on the outside, also formed a circle by joining hands, their arms spread farther apart. Their circle moved counter clockwise. When the music stopped, the man would dance with the woman directly in front of him, and if the couple clicked, they would spend the remainder of the evening dancing together, perhaps exchanging phone numbers, before going back to their gender's quarters, wish each other well, and meet the next morning over breakfast to get to see each other in the honest light of day.

There Was a Beautiful Young Woman ...
On the night of the dance the secretary did her make-up and her hair, put on her favourite skirt, blouse, and a set of pearls her father had given her as a graduation present for her BA, and went to the dance hall with her roommate.

At first both genders were stand-offish, the men clustering in their circles of fishing buddies and pals, and casting glances over at the women in their gatherings. When the master of ceremonies announced, "Paul Jones everyone!" the mood in the room changed. This was the moment that would break the ice for the evening. The women formed their circle and the men formed their outer ring. This was the moment at which chance would enter into the polite social structures of the resort and where chance would dictate who would meet whom and who would dance with whom.

When the music suddenly stopped, the secretary noticed that a dapper though shortish young man hip checked the chap beside him so he could dance with her. He had gleaming blue eyes and he smiled at her. She had the impression he had been watching her earlier in the evening, especially when she left her group and went up to the punch bowl on her own. She also had the strange feeling she had known him all her life and that could be true because Toronto was a place where one passed the same faces every day in the street without asking a person's name.

"May I have this dance with you?" he asked. She smiled and nodded, and he took her left in his right hand and put his left hand around her upper waist. She noted that he wasn't a bad dancer as the "Tennessee Waltz" began and they moved together beneath the big round chandelier. They danced the next dance, and then the next, pausing only to catch their breath on the small lakeside deck off the hall. The lake was alive with stars, and a full moon was just rising over the far shore. They introduced themselves and exchanged telephone numbers, and by the time the evening was almost over they were looking deeply into each other's eyes and exchanging smiles and the promise to breakfast with each other in the morning.

The clock struck midnight, and the dance was over. He walked her back to the women's rooms on the far side of the lodge. Something had happened during their dance. She had the feeling deep inside that she might have found her prince. They said goodnight and went in their opposite directions leaving the rest to chance and the heart. He paused on the walkway and looked down at the ground. It had rained earlier in the evening before the stars came out. There was a footprint in the earth where the stone walk angled away from a flower bed, and he stared at it. Maybe it was her footprint, the image of the shoe she had left behind.

In the morning she was one of the first in the breakfast hall. She looked around anxiously and kept an empty place beside her in the hope that he would show up. He did not. Noon time came and she made inquiries at the front desk about him. "I'm sorry," said the clerk. "He checked out this morning very early. Wait a minute. Yes, he did leave something. He forgot a leather sandal in his room. If you know him or will be seeing him, perhaps you can make sure he gets it back." She was handed a brown paper bag with a single leather sandal inside, its buckle rattling like a tiny bell when she shook it.

Who Met a Handsome Prince ...
Crestfallen, she spent the remainder of the week alone, walking along the lakeside trails, listening to the quiet

chatter of women who had found their princes in the wheel of fortune and feeling as if something had almost started and had been cut short. Her roommate who worked in another office at the Conservatory had met a tall, dark-haired man who occupied her entire time during the week. As for her prince, he had left no message for her, and all she had was the telephone number and the sandal in the brown paper bag. She called her mother in Toronto to ask if the man had telephoned but he had not, and she left instructions as to what her mother was to say to him if he did call.

She returned to the city with nothing to show for her vacation other than a week away and a piece of useless footwear. Her father teased her. "Perhaps you will meet a man with one leg and he will love you for the shoe the other guy lost."

Leaves fell from the trees, and a chill filled the streets of Toronto. The tall sugar maple on her mother's lawn in Lawrence Park suddenly became a gathering of boney hands and empty hopes held up in exasperation to an increasingly grey sky. And as winter gradually settled in and she rode the street car down Yonge each morning, her hopes faded in the silence of another long winter where she would wait and yearn for another week beside the lake in Haliburton, or some other place, where magic might work itself into the plot. And as she rode the street car each day to her desk, she looked at the feet of all the men who got on board and wondered if any of them would fit the errant sandal. There was still no word from the man she had danced with for a single evening and whose charm and grace and deep blue eyes made her feel as if she was floating off the ground and taken up among the stars. But, she tried to tell herself, such things only happen in fairy tales.

The Prince Searched and Searched for Her ...
She had tried, after the appropriate length of time suggested by her mother, to call him, though it was against her mother's better judgement.

"If he is interested in you, let him seek you out. Don't go chasing after him."

"Yes, but I do have his shoe. Well ... it is not entirely a shoe. A lot of it is missing."

"That's his loss," her mother replied.

"Well, maybe it was left for a reason and I should seek him out. It would be a good excuse to call." And call she did, only to find that the number had gone out of service.

"If it was meant to be, it was meant to be," was the guidance her mother proffered. Her mother, like much of Toronto, had been raised in a Presbyterian household where everything was governed by the doctrine of predestination and things that could not be explained happened for a reason, the Good Lord willing.

One night as the snow began to fall, the telephone rang. Her mother picked up the receiver from the black, bell-bottomed phone and handed it to her. "You'd better speak to him. It is the polite thing to do." It was the elusive gentleman she had met at the dance.

After saying hello, he attempted to explain. "I have been trying to reach you. I had to leave early the morning after we danced because my father passed away in the night. I had your number in my summer jacket, but my sister sent it out to be cleaned and the number vanished from the pocket. Then I phone the lodge to see if they would tell me where to find you, and of course they wouldn't because they have a privacy policy and they said if she had wanted to be contacted by me she would have given me her telephone number. I told them about the jacket, and about the house being cleaned out and about the disconnection of my father's number but the whole thing turned into a bramble I couldn't hack my way through."

"So how did you find me?"

"I saw your friend and her boyfriend at a restaurant late one evening. It was near my work. They had been to a movie and were having sandwiches afterwards. I begged them to let me know where to find you. I don't think they remembered me. Well, he remembered me because I pushed him aside to dance with you and all he recalled was that I did something uncharacteristically rude to meet you."

"I have your shoe," she said, "or at least the parts of it you were using last summer."

"Really? How did you come by it?"

"The desk clerk gave it to me. I've been waiting for someone to claim it. Would you like to come by and see if it fits? I mean, it could be someone else's shoe or sandal."

"I'd given up finding the lost one. I had the left in my suitcase. I contacted the lodge several months later and they didn't know what I was talking about so I threw out the left one."

"Do you know any one-legged men?" she said, giggling.

"No, but I do have tickets to the opera for Saturday night and perhaps we can find one there."

And as the young lover, aglow with the footlights

beaming up at him from the streets of an imaginary Paris, sang to a young woman about her frozen hand, the handsome Prince reached over and took hers in his and together their hands grew warm in the cavern of Massey Hall.

And After What Seemed Forever, He Found Her ...

She was extremely disappointed that the flu had ruined their plans for Valentine's Day, but as her fever raged the last thing on her mind was chocolates or a night out. She ached and burned and was not sure whether she was awake or asleep. She dreamed that they were beside the lake again. The stars were glowing and the dancehall was empty except for her and her man and the orchestra who were playing a dance version of "Autumn Leaves." But in her dreams, the leaves were not falling. They were rising from the ground in their brilliant red and orange and glowing yellow and reattaching themselves to the branches of a maple tree like the one on her parent's lawn though in the dream it had sprouted and grown up in the middle of the hardwood floor. And she heard him, she heard the words as real as if he were right beside her, and he was telling her that he loved her and would be true to her forever and that he could not go on with his life alone without her and that he would be the proudest, the happiest man in the world if she would do him the honour of being his wife. And as they were swept upwards into the brilliant pearly sky and the sun and the moon came out to dance together in the amazing purple hue of a magical moment, she felt her mother's hand on her shoulder.

"So what did you say?"

"To who?"

"To him. He was just here with a beautiful red rose and a little box in his other hand."

"Here?"

"Yes. What did you say?"

"To what?"

"He said he proposed."

"I think I said yes."

"You think you said yes? Don't you know?"

"Hey, I've got the flu. I thought I was dreaming, and I think I said yes."

"Well dear," her mother said, "it is times like these when the heart speaks what it really feels."

And the young woman looked at her night-table and a sterling silver box lay beside a glass of orange juice, and on her finger was a diamond ring. At their wedding, the man's brother and best man read a passage from Milton's *Paradise Lost* in which Adam is given the choice of staying on in Eden after the fall, but chooses instead to spend the rest of his days with his Eve, for they "never shall be part-ed, bliss or woe."

And They Lived Happily Ever After ...

My sister and I love to tell our friends the story of how our parents met one September and were married the next on a brilliant day when the valleys of Toronto were adorned in bright yellow golden rod and royal purple asters, and the trees over-arching the boulevards of North Toronto were crimson and gilded.

We also tell our friends how our folks went back to Northern Ireland on one of those "trace your ancestor" trips with a genealogist, and how they discovered that both sides of the family were from County Fermanagh. But it gets more interesting. Both the families had ancestors who came out from Fermanagh to Toronto on sailing ships. Our father's grandfather had travelled with Timothy Eaton who founded the Eaton's department store chain. Our mother's grandmother had travelled with Robert Simpson who founded Simpson's department store, the rival of Eaton's. Our friends ask who we are: Eaton's or Simpson's and we always answer that we grew up in a Morgan's household because that was the closest department store. It is an old Toronto joke about approximations and strange meetings.

But the story of our parents becomes even stranger. Once they reached Fermanagh and had met up with a historian, he showed them where the families had come from. Both were from a little town called Springfield, just outside of Enniskillen. From the ancestral home of our father's family, our parents had looked across a small valley to the ancestral home of our mother's side. And when our intrepid travellers searched the local burial records, they discovered that both sides of the family were buried in a little church yard at a cross-road called Monea. The graves were only a few yards apart, and when our father tripped over a crawling vine that had sprouted from his family's plot, he picked it up and followed it and its end had wrapped itself around the tombstone of our mother's clan.

Everyone, we are told by biologists and anatomists, is the product of chance. Everyone is a longshot miracle where the odds of life play out exactly to code or else we do not exist. That's fact. But there is also truth in fiction and my sister and I saw it one drizzly summer afternoon when she was reading for her doctorate in Dublin and I was researching my post-doc in London. We knew our parents were somewhere in the country, but all we had heard from them in letters was that we would hook up in Dublin when they were done unraveling the mysteries and tangled vines of our ancestry and that we would have one last family holiday together in the Yeats country of County Sligo. They said they would leave word at our B & B about when they would come to Dublin. One of us had sent a letter that caught up with them in Belfast, a short note about our Sligo plans saying "that's no country for old men," to which our father had replied: "Am feeling my oats."

My sister and I had just spent the afternoon in Trinity College Library after meeting up with some friends for a rather wet lunch. As our taxi puttered and halted along Landsdowne Road several blocks from the rooms at our bed and breakfast, we inched along and were discussing the differences between English and Irish literature and wondering where and when we thought our parents might show up. Each of us still had another day's worth of research to do. On the sidewalk about a block ahead of us were two figures—a man and a woman, arm in arm, dressed in navy blue rain hats and navy blue trench coats and sensible brown leather walking shoes. Each had a small brown bag slung over the right shoulder and short umbrellas clutched in their free hands waving back and forth in motion with their stride. They were strolling together, swaying step for step in unison, as if their walk was a dance and each foot forward a bar of music harmonizing with the other.

"Look at those two," I said, pointing them out to my sister. "Maybe they are part of some cult or secret society that makes them dress alike."

"As God made them, he matched them," she said laughing before she stopped herself abruptly and pointed. "O my God! O my God! Look! Those are *our* parents! They're here already!"

And together, as if oblivious to the traffic and the congestion of a Dublin rush hour, we saw them walking together as if attached, as if they were one, swaying with an invisible lilt that connected them to one another. They were two people brought together by the hand of some force that ordained that they should find each other, if not by acquaintance, then by the command of chance. And once together, by the dictates of that mysterious force, they should always be together and live happily ever after. My sister and I agreed that they must have been made for each other and that they reminded us of Adam and Eve at the conclusion of Milton's poem, who through Eden, hand in hand, made their solitary way.

T & C

There are many worlds, some better, some worse, but Mike did not belong in this one. The bright, almost perfectly green pasture hills and their white, horizontal bar fences rolled beautifully toward the shining trees of the wood lot where every inch of growth was tidied of weeds. When held up against the world of Mike's wealthy cousins and their riding crops and sleek black jumping horses, his world of a small apartment and a boring desk job did not stand up well. The only advantage he had over them was that the air of the city streets did not smell of manure.

When they had all been little, his cousins had been as middle class as he was. Maybe they were richer now, but they had sat on the edge of the curb and watched the floats of the Santa Claus Parade pass by; money had not been a dividing line in the extended family. Money was something Mike got for birthdays, and was quietly spirited away by his parents for his college fund. He had been educated. His cousins had not. They didn't need education, his uncle said. Their side of the family came into wealth.

Uncle Garry loved to go to Kentucky. "The horses are fast and the women are faster," he liked to quip, and he should have lost at least half his fortune to Aunt Martha in the divorce. Martha never spoke up at family gatherings. She sat with her hands folded on her lap, clearing her throat, and nodding whenever Garry spoke.

"Lucky for me, she died of cancer," Uncle Garry chuckled to Mike from behind the lavish mahogany bar in the stud-farm's family room. Garry poured a bourbon for each of them. Matilda, the jumper cousin, lounged on one arm on the leather sofa. She set her feet up on the coffee table. Between the heel and the sole of her right riding boot, a small clump of horse cookie hung on for dear life, and the smell reminded everyone in the room that she had come from the paddock.

Handing his nephew the drink, Uncle Garry looked into his with a profound, philosophical gaze as if he was thinking of something important to say. Whenever his uncle did that, something stupid usually came out. Uncle Garry had made a lot of money in the land flip business.

"This stuff will kill you," he said, looking up and laughing at his own joke and poking a finger at Mike. "So Mike, you're all grown up now. Finished a business degree. Got your own place, and all. I betcha got a good view from that condo."

Mike thought for a moment. It was a rented condo, but he always felt nervous around his uncle and didn't want to fix the broken fact. He nodded. In his mind the view, not a bad view for downtown, looked into another condo across the narrow street that had only recently been made out of the old rail lands. If he leaned from the tiny, two-chair balcony, far enough out to see but not so far as to lose his balance and fall from the sixteenth floor, he could see the lake. One Sunday morning, when he dared the view, the lake had been blue and sparkling. The rest of the time he never bothered to look. It was either too windy or he was too busy.

Mike said: "Yes sirree, a good view. I can see the lake. Can't see much else."

Mike decided not to tell his uncle about the Chinese girl. She lived directly across from him. One winter night, just a few months ago, he and the Chinese girl had the lights on late in their own little boxes, and Mike realized that neither wanted or could afford a decent set of drapes to shut the world off from the small quarters of their lives.

He had gone to the window to stare at the other buildings, to see if anyone would stare back. The girl had pushed her desk up against the sliding balcony door. Obviously, she wasn't an out-doorsy type, or maybe during the day if she was home she preferred natural light to the artificial kind. Whatever the case, Mike had seen her. He stared for several minutes. People when they are being watched quickly get the sense that someone is looking at them. Mike loved sixth-sense games.

She looked up and saw him. Mike waved. She immediately stood up from her desk and turned off the lights.

Matilda lifted her feet off the coffee table. Mike was relieved he didn't have to look at horse crap any more. She reached across the table and grabbed a copy of *Town and Country*.

"I'm in this issue," she said as she tossed it to Mike. "Take it. There's more where that came from. You can read all about my horsey life." She got up and went to the bar and started reading the bottles as if they were a library shelf.

Garry said: "Yep, that was a great shoot they did last summer. The photographers, the light guys. They did a video, and all the stills. Hundreds of stills. Matty with the horse. Matty without the horse. Matty with the estate in the background. Matty in a deb dress, though she's way beyond that. Then this French guy with a camera says: 'Let's get some action shots. Jump your horse over one of the fences.'"

"Bad idea," Matilda interjected.

"I shoulda said something, but I'd had a few with the light guy when we'd got to talking about the big white disk he was carrying around, so I brought him in and we had some more."

Matilda spoke up. "What Daddy is about to tell you is that the photographer didn't like the actual practice rails in the side paddock because you could see the concession way off in the background, and they were doing some road work, and making dust smoke, so he tells me to jump Custer. You know Custer? He was the one I rode in the provincials last year. He tells me to jump Custer over one of the fences in the main paddock. I said no, and he said: 'I see a cover shot.' And the cover shot thing got the best of me."

Garry said: "The bugger didn't get his shot. I had to have one of our best horses put down. Custer's last stand, if you know what I mean. Matty broke her shoulder."

"Collarbone, Dad, collarbone. Not fun."

"Fucking photographer."

Mike said: "You're okay now? Right?"

"It ruined my two months in Barbados."

Garry spoke up again. "Enough, kitten. I got a question for Mike. Mike, my boy, you seem pretty enterprising. Would you like to come and work for me in my business? I need a regional manager for the northern territory."

"The north? How far north?"

"All the other regions, well you know, I've got my gang, and all the other regions are fixed up right now. Not Arctic. We're talking about near north. Sort of resorts, and lakes, and condos on lakes. That sort of thing."

Mike's hands parted and his palms turned upward. "Yeah, I'm interested. Can I think about it? Not long, but I'd like to think about it. It's a great offer. I guess salary comes with it sort of like ..."

Garry roared and looked at Matilda. "The little snipe wants to be paid! Waddya think of that, eh kitten? He wants to be paid. Yep, we can pay you. We'll talk about that if you're interested."

Mike returned to the city. He stood in his darkened apartment, staring at the city lights and thinking about what he should do. The firm he was with now had hired him at a university job fair. He'd lined up with all the others, the hundreds of others, the ones who didn't not get a job at the fair.

"You're our man," his boss had told him. "You have a future."

Mike just didn't know. He felt uneasy at the prospect of change, and worst of all, at the idea of working for his uncle. He knew too much about his uncle to be comfortable with it.

As he looked up, Mike saw the Chinese girl in the window. She was switching her desk lamp on and off to get his attention. When she was certain he had seen her, she left the lamp on and waved back.

Mike waved, too.

She pointed down, and kept pointing down, until Mike realized that she wanted him to go down to the street. He gave her a thumbs up.

The night was cool for a spring evening, but the road was shining and reflected the sodium vapour street lamps in the damp from a rain that had fallen earlier in the evening. His breath hung in front of him as he stood waiting on the sidewalk. The girl approached.

"I'm sorry I was rude to you back a few months ago when you waved. It startled me. You don't expect to see another soul looking out their window in the middle of the night. I'm Sharon."

"Mike," he said as they shook hands. "Want to get a coffee?"

"Tea'd be nicer."

"Tea it is then." And they walked around the corner to an all-night doughnut place haunted by insomniacs. Mike went there often.

Sharon said: "I've seen you here. I usually sit at the back so I can watch people coming and going and not be seen. You usually sit in the window as if you are waiting for someone or something that never arrives."

"Never does," Mike said.

"Let's talk about it," Sharon said.

The sky was becoming pale-blue in the east as they headed back to their buildings. They'd been talking all night. Mike told her what he waited for when he sat in the window. "The future," he said.

"I know what you mean," Sharon replied.

They'd talked of their school years, their university years. She'd studied out of town. He'd studied in town because he couldn't afford the residence fees. They talked about what they wanted, and how Mike had just been offered a job by his uncle, and he didn't know because he thought the guy was a crook and a bastard, a spoiled bastard, and he felt his current job was a dead-end. Her job was like that, too. It was a "McJob," she said and shook her head.

"You know, when you're a kid you think you're going to make it big, you're going to be the star of the show because that's what life teaches you," Sharon said. "It tells you you have to shine. I got pushed by my parents. I love them, they want me to be a success, and I guess that's their way of showing love, but my mother said to me that she didn't raise me to work in an office even if I have four people working under me, and that I'd failed. It's awful. That pressure."

Mike nodded.

They agreed to go for dinner and a movie, or a movie and dinner. It didn't matter what order, the following night. That's when they began to be Mike and Sharon.

Every night they would flash their lights at each other before they went to sleep if they weren't in his place together or her place together.

Garry called one night when they were watching a movie on Mike's laptop and cuddling together with a bowl of popcorn on the couch.

"Heard you have a girl friend, hey guy? Bet she's a hot one. That job is still on the table but I need an answer soon."

Mike said he was still thinking about it, but he wasn't sure he wanted to be on the road now that he was in a relationship.

"Well get back to me soon, fella," Garry said as he hung up.

One Sunday afternoon when they were downtown window-shopping together, Sharon's mother spotted them.

"Oh, my God," Sharon said, almost frantic and in tears as she sat with Mike at her desk and shut the lid on her laptop before the movie was even half-way through. "She's livid. I can't keep it inside. She's angry at me. She was screaming at me: 'No white boy! No white boy!' She's old-fashioned. I told her I'd choose who I want. That's sacrilege, Mike, sacrilege."

They held each other. Neither knew what to do.

Garry called Mike at his office the next day.

"I saw you with that girl on the weekend. Yeah, yeah, I get around. Guy, let me tell you, she's not worth it. If that's what's holding you up, I'm afraid I gotta get someone else. Sorry buddy, but time moves on. Time is money."

Mike sat in silence. That night he told Sharon.

"We're fucked, but we might as well make our own ways. If we're going to be on our own, so be it. These are our lives. I love you."

"I love you, too," she said, tears welling up in her eyes as she tried to smile.

"We're in the dark, but we found each other in the dark, and maybe that's what's meant to be. I don't see us together in a grand estate out in the country. I don't see us in our little condo apartments either. I just see us together. Let's make our own way."

Mike gave up his place and they moved in to her place that was equally tiny. They saved every dollar they could. There were married at City Hall, and had a party for their friends at an Italian restaurant in the west end of the downtown.

Neither Sharon's parents nor Uncle Garry and the cousins would attend.

A few years later, they had saved enough for a starter-home down payment. They would ride the packed commuter train into the city, past the houses crammed together on nameless side streets, and past the cemeteries pressing against the right of way with rows of white and grey headstones that reminded them of teeth.

Their home was out on the edge of the developments where house farms sprang from the old fields and estates that had once been beyond the point that their friends called civilization.

"Are you happy here?" Mike asked Sharon one night as they lay together in bed.

"Yes, very. This is probably the first time in my life I've been happy."

"Me, too. What makes happiness happen?"

Sharon thought for a moment. "Happiness is how we sustain ourselves. I think we're still hunter-gatherers. I remember thinking that in an elective anthropology class at university. But instead of gathering food, we gather what we need. Those who over eat, who acquire more and more or demand that others acquire more and more, well, they're gluttons. Their food supply won't be there some-day. Us? We gather what we need. I've got all I need, and that's what makes me happy. I've got you. The baby on the way. A job. A roof over our heads. It is a veritable feast. We're lucky."

"Yes, I think we are. Thank you for doing this with me. Thank us for doing it together. For the first time in my life, I can see the future. I never was able to see it before. Someone always tried to point me to something else, something away from what I thought I saw. But I see it now."

They rolled over and held each other, their breaths and even their heartbeats in sync. They stared into each other's eyes. They listened to the sound of the night, the crickets in the late summer at the end of their garden where the world of the town and the world of the country met in their truce. They were the no-man's land. They were the past on the verge of the future. Their house, their world together, was a bulwark against both town and country.

It was a small house, but it was an investment, and it was theirs. For a few years, before the world of avenues and addresses pushed the town farther and farther into the country, they would sit at the table in the dark of their kitchen and stare out the sliding glass door onto a deck just large enough for a barbecue.

Beyond the deck, beyond their garden that was not yet fenced, and beyond the wood lot in the distance where they gathered red and gold autumn leaves to decorate their Thanksgiving table, they would watch the sky grow brighter and brighter out of the darkness until they were certain it was dawn.

Acknowledgements

The author would like to thank David Moratto for his splendid design and loving detail to type and cover image. A very special thank you to Michael Mirolla of Guernica Editions for his careful eye and his patience in the production of this book. Thank you to Karen Wetmore of Grenville Printing at Georgian College for her assistance with countless requests for xeroxes of these stories as this book evolved, and to Professor Rich Butler of McMaster University for hosting me during the Whidden Lectures many years ago. And thank you to Margaret Meyer, Dr. Carolyn Meyer, Katie Meyer, my wife Kerry Johnston, and my writing companion, Daisy, for their support and encouragement with this book.

About the Author

Writer, editor, educator, photographer, poet, broadcaster, and storyteller, Bruce Meyer is author or editor of more than sixty books of poetry, short fiction, non-fiction, memoir, literary journalism and pedagogy. His most recent books include the anthologies *Cli-Fi: Canadian Tales of Climate Change*, *That Dammed Beaver: Canadian Laughs, Gaffes, and Humour;* the reissue/reconstruction of the lost World War One novel, *Cry Havoc* (by W. Redvers Dent), and the poetry collections *The Seasons* (which won the IP Medal for best book of poems published in North America and runner-up for the Cogswell Prize for Poetry), *1967: Centennial Year, The Arrow of Time* (finalist for the Raymond Souster Prize), *Testing the Elements, The Madness of Planets,* and *To Linares* (published in Mexico in both English and Spanish). His work has been translated in Korean, Bangla, Spanish, Danish, French, Italian, and Chinese. His national bestsellers include *The Golden Thread: A Reader's Journey Through the Great Books* and *Portraits of Canadian Writers.* He lives in Barrie, Ontario, with his wife, CBC journalist Kerry Johnston and their daughter, Katie. He was the inaugural Poet Laureate of the City of Barrie, and teaches at Georgian College and at Victoria College in the University of Toronto.